Core Samples

Core Samples

by

Patti Grayson

TURNSTONE PRESS

Turnstone Press
Artspace Building
607-100 Arthur Street
Winnipeg, MB
R3B 1H3 Canada
www.TurnstonePress.com

Turnstone Press gratefully acknowledges the assistance of The Canada
Council for the Arts, the Manitoba Arts Council, the Government of
Canada through the Book Publishing Industry Development Program
and the Government of Manitoba through the Department of Culture,
Heritage and Tourism, Arts Branch, for our publishing activities.

The Canada Council | Le Conseil des Arts
for the Arts | du Canada

MANITOBA arts COUNCIL
CONSEIL DES DU MANITOBA

Canadä

Cover design: Doowah Design
Interior design: Sharon Caseburg
Printed and bound in Canada by Friesens for Turnstone Press.

A version of "Jackpot Jungle" originally appeared in Prairie Fire; "Too
Much Beauty . . . Is Curse" in *Under the Prairie Sky Anthology*; and
"What Jeanie and Ella Canned" in *Other Voices*.

National Library of Canada Cataloguing in Publication Data

Grayson, Patti, 1957-

  Core samples / by Patti Grayson.

ISBN 0-88801-294-2

  I. Title.

PS8613.R39C67 2004   C813'.6   C2004-900951-6

For my family

Contents

Core Samples

Love's Little Surprise

IT WAS SUCH A SURPRISE TO SEE IT THERE. AS I ROUNDED THE last blind curve on River Road, it sat right in the centre, as if someone had stepped out and placed it on the solid yellow double line. A ladies' hat. Not your discount store variety of cheap beige straw and polka dot band, but a lovely hat: a cool coral straw with a matching satin band, the brim turned down, a style for ladies who don't ordinarily look good in hats, but who can put one like that on their heads and know they will be enviable in it. I surmised this in the time it took my foot to hit the brake pedal. A reflex response. I felt silly braking for a hat, but I had the overwhelming feeling that inside the hat there would still be a head, detached from the rest of its body, hiding under the wide, turned-down brim. And as illogical as it seemed, the image of my mother's head flashed into my mind. To my knowledge, Mother didn't own such a hat. Though I'm certain she would have gushed over it at the milliner's and paid any price that was being asked. It was the kind of hat she could have worn to my father's wedding that day, if she had been inclined to be less bitter about the whole thing. Being fair to her, I

didn't suppose that women often attended their ex-husbands' sub-
sequent weddings, but six years had passed since my parents'
divorce and Mother still referred to him only if it was necessary,
and then not by his name, Nate—but as "your father."

I swerved to the side of the road, and stepped out of my car. A
meadowlark trilled. The river alongside me wound its way
around the bend. It was an exceptional blue under the bright
morning sunshine and cloudless sky. A flawless day for Father
and Bernadette's wedding. The hat was back fifty feet, and as I
walked towards it, I thought it looked rather bold lying there . . .
like a sunbather, who has undone her bikini top and demands pri-
vacy. It was evident, from my bizarre thoughts, that visiting
Mother that morning was filling me with trepidation. I was try-
ing to be thoughtful by visiting her (or was I trying to assuage my
guilt for agreeing to be Bernadette's attendant)? Either way, I
should have been at Bernadette's side by that time, gushing over
her hairstyle and the way her headpiece adorned her head. It
would have been the better choice than trying to have Mother
not feel left out on that June morning.

I was ten feet away when the breeze off the river gusted and
picked the hat up. It tumbled over itself, caught in the long grass
along the river, then lifted free, blew in a great charge and cas-
caded down onto the water. It floated, a cool, coral defiance,
accepting only the current's direction. It would only be a matter
of time before the river swallowed it. If it travelled as far as the
locks, it would become embroiled in the river's desire to re-estab-
lish rapids there, and be churned into shredded straw. I turned
away from it, overwhelmed with a sadness I couldn't explain.

A few minutes later I turned into my mother's driveway. She'd
kept the house and everything in it. Once I'd moved out on my
own, I thought perhaps it would be wise for Mother to do the
same, that she should move into the city, take a luxury condo, a
memory-free environment. Instead, she spent money fixing the
house I grew up in, making improvements, gutting the kitchen,
adding new gardens. Father paid. She said she loved that house. I
wondered if she loved it more than she loved him.

Mother did not answer when I opened the front door and called her name. As I passed through the living room, I noticed that her curio cabinet was empty and the top of the mantel was bare. Curious. I went through to the kitchen and saw her out on the deck. I had been thinking of telling her about the hat, but the thought was wiped from my mind when I joined her outside. She was surrounded by her Lladró porcelain figurines; some resting on the deck, some standing on the patio table, some lying on the lawn on their sides. Others were stacked on top of each other in a box she'd used to transport them, without a single sheet of tissue or newspaper to separate and protect them from one another.

"Mother, what in the world . . . ?"

"Oh Cassandra, I didn't hear you arrive, darling." She stood up and gave me a hug. She smelled so good. Mother always did. Even to the corner store, she wore perfume. You never caught my mother naked of scent.

"Mother, what are you doing?"

"It was too fine a morning to be inside dusting, but I really felt the need to take care of these today, so I decided to kill two birds with one stone, so to speak, and bring them outside to clean them."

"But Mother, the ones in the box . . . and the wind."

Mother's Lladró figurines were her favourite things. She had crystal, silver, oil paintings and exotic jade carvings, but nothing compared to her porcelain figurines. As a child, I was not allowed to so much as touch a single one of them. Sometimes, when Mother was in a generous mood, and there were no pressing parties or social events to organize, she would take them out one by one and show them to me. "*Look, but don't touch, Cassandra,*" she would say and then recite their names and describe how she'd come to attain each one of them—the majority of them gifts from my father. Their elongated, pale figures resembled my mother. Slender and ethereal. Muted grey, taupe and blue elegance.

Mother smiled at me as I pointed at the precariousness of her most prized possessions.

"They'll be fine, Cassandra, just fine. Have you had your coffee?"

"I'm staying clear of caffeine right now, Mother," I said, but I could not take my eyes off the jumble of *Girl with Geese* lying on top of *Dancer*, *Swan Ballet* and *Opening Night*, which in turn were on top of *Merry Ballet* and *Before the Dance*—all of her dancers in a heap.

"I'll get you some nice ice water with lemon," Mother added and waltzed off to the kitchen, as cool as the breeze fluttering the petals off the peonies beside me.

I picked up the nightgowned *Girl with Candle* and remembered the day Mother wept when the flame snapped off the candle of her original figure. Unknown to my parents, I had been jumping on their bed that evening while the babysitter they'd hired had been talking on the phone, and although I never heard the figure fall or witnessed its smashing, I considered it my fault. When my parents returned from their party late that night, I heard Mother weeping over the broken figurine. They never accused me of breaking it, but that particular babysitter was never hired again. My father removed the broken figurine from our home and a few months later, he returned from business in Spain with a perfect, new replacement. "Directly from the source to your front door," he'd said with a flourish when he presented Mother with it. Then he also produced *Bedtime Story*, a mother and daughter figurine she had been coveting. She had thrown her arms around him and squealed with delight. I skipped around my parents in a circle, glad to be unburdened of my guilt; so very thankful to Father for such an extraordinary feat.

"Would you like to have that one?" Mother asked as she came out with a tray of warm muffins and lemon ice water.

Still holding *Girl with Candle*, I frowned at her, confused. Then realizing that she must be beside herself over Father's wedding, I tried to cajole her. "What's this?" I asked. "You're going to part with one of these while you're still living and breathing on this earth?" I placed the smooth, porcelain coolness to my cheek.

She frowned back at me and sniffed. There was an awkward

silence. She had taken offense, and I sighed. I tried to make amends. "That's very generous, Mother, but I'd hate to break up the collection. Besides, I always enjoy coming home for inspection. It wouldn't be the same if I owned one of them." I paused as she poured out two tall glasses, then I added, "You really should consider insuring them. There have been so many break-ins lately."

"I'm having new deadbolts installed, Cassandra. Now, I'll just have to remember to lock them. When we first moved here, no one secured their doors." Mother paused to take a sip of her water and brush a wisp of stray hair from her forehead before she added, "Times have changed."

I couldn't help gulping my water. I wanted to tell Mother that I had never tasted better water, not from a bottle, not from any mountain springs, not anywhere I'd ever travelled, but it wasn't enough, somehow, to compliment her on the water that was merely pumped up from the well. It was not going to make up for the years I'd blamed her for divorcing Father. I never came out and told her to her face, but I spent my later teenage years slamming doors and refusing to join her at the dinner table. I suppose I might have done that anyway, to both of them, but under the circumstances I directed all my fury at her and her decision.

Mother interrupted my thoughts, "Well, pick one, dear. Weren't you always partial to *In the Gondola*? She got up from her seat and from another box procured the figurine. It almost took my breath away each time I saw it. The long gondola boat, the gondolier poling down the canal, the couple in their Sunday finery facing their only child, a lovely young girl, perhaps her first holiday on the Continent. It was how I envisioned our family in my most romantic thoughts. And even though Father never took us on his business travels, I always assumed that we would go to Venice some day, and there we'd be, just like *In the Gondola*.

"Mother? What has got into you this morning?" I blurted, annoyance creeping into my voice. Why did she have to be acting so strangely? Father had been living with Bernadette for three years already; their wedding was only a formality. I stopped myself and said calmly, "Why don't you tell me the story of where that one came from, Mother?"

She looked at me. She sipped her water and looked out towards the river. I shifted in my chair. She set down her water glass.

"Cassandra, now that your father's happiness is about to become official, perhaps you should hear the real story of how I got *In the Gondola* and so many of the others. Let's see, *In the Gondola*, your father's version: Ah yes, well he was in Italy of course that spring and although he didn't get to Venice, he saw this piece in the window of a small curiosity shop in Rome, down a narrow side street. The family who had sold it to the shop owner had been down on their luck or something. Your father bought it for a song. The only second-hand piece he'd ever purchased, according to the story. In mint condition, of course.

"Now, if my memory serves me correctly, Louanna, the redhead, was his secretary at the time. I believe she went to Rome with him . . . saw works by Michelangelo, I imagine, and had to ask your father who that was." Mother stopped. "Never mind, Cassandra, never mind."

I was having difficulty swallowing. There was a silence punctuated by a meadowlark's trilling. It sounded harsh and cacophonous. "There was someone before Bernadette?" I had always assumed that Father's business life, his being away constantly, Mother on her own with me, were the reasons she'd divorced him.

Mother laughed.

I flushed, feeling suddenly like the naive child who'd jumped on their bed that night. "Continue, please!" I insisted.

"Bernadette must be a very special woman for your father to have stayed with her this long, Cassandra. I thought after the divorce, he'd know better than to tie himself to one woman, but she seems to have found the recipe for success. Or perhaps she's able to look the other way. I did. For years."

"Why?" I was furious with my mother all over again. All the years of blaming her were instantly turned around, but now I was livid with her for admitting to staying with my father after he'd had affairs.

Mother must have seen the fury in my face. "It wasn't the affairs, though God knows I have to admit I told myself a lot of lies to get past them," she said quietly. "No, it was Bernadette, actually. She was unlike the others. She left your father's employ when he found a reason—a younger blonde perhaps—to encourage her to find employment elsewhere, and I suppose she really loved him. Really loved him. Because she came to me after his new secretary was hired and she told me the truth about the figurines. She informed me that Mildred—a woman in Accounting, who had worked for your father from the first months of the company—was the person who bought them. Mildred had an entire file drawer in her office, brimming with catalogues and leaflets and lists of dealers in the country and beyond. She was the one who chose them, walked downtown to purchase the local ones, ordered the numerous more exotic ones long-distance, wrapped them and always had one ready for your father's return from a trip so that he could wind some yarn about how he came to purchase it during his travels, as if my concerns were his concerns while he was away. As if he really cared about me, took time out from his business matters especially to please me. All the while, it was Mildred. Dear woman, she must have been more besotted with your father than any of us to take part in such a deception. Or perhaps she just loved the figurines as much as I did?"

"Oh, Mother," I squeaked out my indignation.

She looked at me and smiled, then relaxed. "That's why I divorced your father. Over the Lladró lies." She swept her arm in a wide arc, indicating the figurines that surrounded her. "Perhaps Bernadette was more calculating than I give her credit for. She had your father crawling back to her somehow, and she had an accurate sense of how to eliminate me." Mother shook her head, looked back out to the river.

"Anyway, Cassandra, darling, that's all in the past. Now, I have a wedding gift for your father and Bernadette. I've wrapped up

Love's Little Surprise to give to them. Would you run upstairs to my dresser, retrieve it, and take it to them for me?"

"Mother, why would …? Is that appropriate?"

"What could be more appropriate? I bought that one myself. Hush, Cassandra, just go get it, like a good girl, will you?"

My mother's room is the very expression of femininity. Pretty chintz fabrics and silk gossamer. I found the wrapped package on her dresser, which was bare of the several special figurines she had kept there. *Romeo and Juliet*, who leaned on their ivy column with so much longing in their long bodies. *Happy Anniversary*, his gift on their final anniversary, the one he'd brought home three days late. Mother had reached up for a kiss in just the same way as the figurine after she'd opened it. *Girl with Candle* had been relegated to the glass cabinet downstairs after her incident and subsequent replacement. I picked up the gift-wrapped box and imagined *Love's Little Surprise* inside. The male holding a package behind his back and the female's delicate hand reaching for it. I was thinking all this when I heard, through the open window, the first of the smashing. I ran to the window and saw Mother standing by the large rock that dominated the river's edge. She was throwing the figurines at it, two at a time. The pieces flew up in a shower, some landing in the river, others spraying back towards the lawn.

I bent down and screamed through the screen. "Mother!"

She turned her head to look. She saw me in her window, and there was a slight pause before she waved and turned back to her efforts. By the time I ran down the stairs and out the door, more than a dozen of them had been smashed and Mother was headed back to the patio to refill the box.

"Mother, stop it!" I demanded.

Mother paused, set the box down on the lawn and said, "Did you think you'd inherit them, Cassandra?"

It was the cruellest thing my mother had ever said to me. If she'd hauled off and punched me in the jaw, I would have been less surprised. Mother set back to refilling the box. I watched *Sea Breeze* with her wind-swept stance roll off *Petals on the Wind* to land on the bottom of the box. It was breaking my heart to see them like that, but I did nothing to stop her. Mother proceeded back to the rock and I saw the head of *Lady in Love* skip off the rock and splash into the river. That was the same moment Mother spotted the hat. She squatted down at the river's edge, amidst the broken pieces of porcelain, and reached into the water for the coral object. She lifted it out of the water, shook the Red River off, then she held it at arm's length and took a good look at it. A small laugh caught in my throat at the thought of it floating so far and coming to no harm. Mother walked back slowly towards me, and said, "Cassandra, look what I've found."

Bring to Bear

THAT'S RIGHT ... LOOK STRAIGHT AT ME, BUT YOU CAN'T SEE ME through the store-front plate-glass because it's too bright out there in the scorching sun, isn't it, Wally Grift? I'm scoped on you, though. Sights set. Crosshairs lined up on your stringy, greying hair. You can't see the barrel pointed at you. You're going to saunter down the street to the bank, your beer belly offering some shade for your boots. You're going to act as guiltless as the day is long, as if your only crime today is not plugging the parking meter, as if you don't have anything that doesn't belong to you. Pull your greasy ball cap down lower to shade your squinting eyes; stop to snuff your roll-your-own, grinding your boot into the soft asphalt. I wish that cigarette butt was your face, Wally Grift, you—to use one of Grandpa's expressions—fat wart on a skunk's reeking arse.

"What you doing, Lainie?" Ray calls from behind the cash register counter. He's stringing bobbers on the fishing line that hangs from the ceiling. I should have noticed the bobbers needed restocking and taken care of that, but I've been too preoccupied this morning. Ray chooses a smaller size bobber—up the line from largest to smallest—and continues talking. "You wanna put one of those on layaway for the fall? I finally convince you that with the bears, you shouldn't be living out there without a gun?"

"I told you, Ray," I say, my eye still trained through the scope. "I don't have any trouble with bears."

"Nobody asks for trouble with bears, Lainie," Ray says. "Maybe you've got no trouble right now ... there are lots of berries this year. But there were berries the year that ol' bear came through your grandma's kitchen screen door ... your grandpa and me off giving your dad his first duck-hunting lesson ... your grandma just crazy enough to try and defend herself with a broom against that beady-eyed misbegotten. Damn near destroyed the kitchen. Your grandma was never the same after that male bear waltzed in. She spent way too much time at her loom. And what are you going to do, Lainie, if big bruin comes through the new patio screen smacking its lips? Sit it down and teach it to weave placemats?"

Lowering the rifle, I look over at Ray.

He continues talking. "I know your grandpa trained Shale. Lord knows I felt the power of that pup through the guard arm! I've worn that protective sleeve for a few of your grandpa's dogs over the years, and maybe it's just my age, but Shale damn near gave me a heart attack when he latched onto it. But even a Schutzhund-trained German shepherd's no match against a bear, Lainie."

"Ray, I don't need a gun. I don't want a gun! And I would never shoot a badass bear, even if I had one."

Ray's arms hang in mid-air. He fumbles with a bobber, drops it, stoops to pick it up. His face is reddened when he straightens again. "Gee, Lainie, you know I was just saying, eh?" I find a dust rag and start working on the barrels of the shotguns. Before I can apologize for snapping at Ray, he's explaining himself. "Damn gun legislation must be getting to me. Worried about fall sales this year. You know hunting season's my bread and butter, Lainie, and I have to think about retiring soon." He offers a self-deprecating laugh.

I sigh. I'm one of the biggest reasons Ray is worried about business. I've been on his payroll since last fall, since I came back for Grandpa's funeral. Ray was the one who told me that my parents had called from where they're living in Arizona to say they couldn't afford the trip back for the funeral since Grandpa had willed the place to me. And Ray was there a few hours before the funeral when my boyfriend, Darrel, called long-distance from our apartment on the coast and said, in his overtly intellectual way, *Your grandfather's passing has provided me with the opportunity to assess our future together, and I think we should call it quits, Lainie.* I guess Ray felt sorry for me—maybe always felt sorry for me, the way my parents would drift off *looking to make a go of things,* leaving me with my grandparents more often than not—because Ray said he could use a hand at the store, if I wanted to stay home for a while. I must have felt sorry for myself too, because instead of delivering an appropriate response to Darrel such as, *My grandfather's passing has provided me with the opportunity to assess you as an asshole,* I placed the phone back on the receiver and accepted Ray's offer . . . just until I could start a little business with Grandma's loom, maybe sell homemade woven crafts. Eventually, with some luck and clever marketing, I could expand the business back to the coast. Winter is Ray's slow season; he couldn't really afford to keep me on the payroll. Since then my own inertia has combined with small-town stagnation. I can't motivate myself to find another job; I've yet to finish a set of placemats. I'm continuing in a uniform straight motion until some force knocks me off course. I wonder if today's the day.

To bolster Ray's spirits, I set down the dust rag and say, "This is a gun-crazy town. Government legislation won't stop anybody in Hematite from buying a gun, except for maybe Gunther-on-parole. Of course, he's always good for a few B & E's before he goes back in. Insurance companies will be buying a few guns to replace the ones he steals. It's all good for business. Hey, Ray, I heard Coffee Catch installed an iced cappuccino machine. My treat?" I point to the door.

"I'll give one of them a try. Thanks, Lainie," Ray says and his face brightens.

I check my pocket to make sure I have enough change. "Back in five," I say to Ray, then step out of the air-conditioning. The heat hits like a fist in the face.

I cross the street straight to Wally Grift's truck. If Shale is in there in this temperature, I'll go back and load that .303; take aim at the exact place where Grift's shirt buttons are taxed beyond their plastic capacity. To think that one summer, when I was about eight, I imagined I would marry Wally Grift ... the leathery, sinewy bachelor from down my grandparents' beach, who was several years older than my dad, and who handled a motorboat as if it were an extension of his body, earning big American tips from being a fishing and hunting guide. I cringe, looking back. Often, when I pressed my childhood nose up against the glass of the adult world, I couldn't see right ...screened by my own naivety. Darrel flashes into my head; is it possible my naive screen is still in place?

Inside Grift's truck cab are the remnants of a takeout chicken dinner. Two flies are crawling over batter crumbs. Another one buzzes the passenger's window and one hovers around the empty two-four case behind the seat. I'm about to walk away when I see it. Shale's collar. A flash of blue nylon on the floor. I cup my hands around my eyes to see inside more clearly. I don't care who's watching me crane my neck like this. I was right. Goddamn Wally Grift has my dog. That was Shale barking from inside Grift's shack this morning. He's also removed the tags from the collar: the thin proof that she's now mine. Sweat breaks out on the back of my neck and trickles under my shirt. I can almost feel the weight of Shale's head on my lap the day of Grandpa's funeral. I'd gone back to the cabin and built a fire in the grate, not bothering to remove my suit skirt. I sat down on the hearthrug to warm my legs and Shale slunk over on his belly, licked my hand once, and put his head on my lap. He looked up with those sad, chocolaty eyes and sighed the biggest dog sigh I'd ever heard, as if to say, "What's to become of me now, Lainie?" . . . the last of the strays and pound dogs to have my grandpa imprinted on their loyal hearts.

The iced cappuccinos drip a stream of condensation by the

time I return to Ray with them. The store exhales cool air, but I'm wavering in a heat haze of desperate thoughts. I see Grift's truck pull away from the curb, and I go back to the gun section. I open a box of .303 cartridges ...the circular brass bottoms, the shiny casings, the discipline of their rows, their uniformity, their inert harmlessness, their lethal potential. The cappuccino leaves a wet ring on the glass counter above the boxes of bullets and shells. I imagine a circular hole in Grift's chest; contemplating that of which I am incapable.

I catch Ray watching me. I should tell him about Shale, but the first thing he'll do is dial the cops. Ray, who was my grandpa's best friend for their whole adult lives, is blessed. He sees things that are broken and he fixes them; he sees things that are wrong and believes they will be righted. I am forever plagued by nuance and subtleties, certain in my pessimism. Ray wouldn't see the fact that the police chief receives his firewood, split and delivered for free from Wally Grift, as an impediment to justice. Plus, Ray can't see what's in my head: a guy who's now a corporal on the force offering me a ride home from a baseball dance the summer we were both seventeen—after we'd swayed the last dance together, slow and charged. Ray can't hear him calling me a cocktease when he sidetracked to the gravel pits and I wouldn't climb in the back seat with him. *Good thing I've got a right hand, Lainie*, he growled. I remember the hostile greenish glow of the dash lights, the stench of his pine air freshener mingling with the couple of underage beers on his breath as he sped back into town. I am forever turning away from that memory in my head . . . and that is not the only one. Even with Darrel, overtly intellectual Darrel, there was the opportunity to feel inadequate; the way he dangled the little bag from the sex shop, as if what was inside was really a gift for me.

Ray reports that he could take a liking to iced cappuccinos, and then suggests I shove off for the afternoon. "It's too hot not to be down by the lake relaxing," he says.

"Are you sure, Ray?" I say, trying not to sound too anxious about getting out of there. I have to rescue Shale somehow. Maybe Grift's not going straight home.

My hand cranks the back door handle of the store as Ray stops me. "By the way, Lainie, I suppose I should have done something about this before now. You know, your grandpa kept a loaded rifle in the house for umpteen years after the bear incident. Taught your grandmother how to use it."

I nod. "I know. He even taught me how to target practise with a .22 the summer I turned twelve."

Ray smiles. "I forgot about that! That was the summer your grandpa grumbled about keeping you in ammo. I had to reorder stock twice, if memory serves me . . . until you accidentally shot that . . . was it a squirrel or a chipmunk?"

I stare at Ray.

He turns away and looks around the partition wall to see if anyone has come into the store. "Anyway, when the government passed Bill C-68, your grandpa said he wasn't registering any of his guns. He hid them, instead. Just before he died, he told me they were mine to sell as used if I could. I didn't get around to collecting them. But you should know you're harbouring illegal weapons in the back bedroom closet under a couple of loose floorboards. Ammunition is in a tin box down there too."

I look at Ray. "You should come over sometime soon and collect those."

Ray nods his head. "I should."

The steering wheel of Grandpa's old jeep burns my fingers. I roll down the windows and wonder if the heat could prevent me from swinging an axe . . . turning Grift's door into firewood to get Shale out.

Three months earlier, Grift had uttered a threat against Shale: I'd been dozing in the late afternoon sun, the first hot day of spring, the lake still too cold to swim in, the floating dock rocking beneath me, the sound of a water bomber thrumming through the cloudless but smoke-hazed sky en route to a forest fire further north. Shale was lying under the shade of a cedar. He rose and barked, but I didn't see Grift until he was on the dock. His boots thumped on the boards as he came towards me. Shale lay back down.

Grift said, "Well, lookee here. We've got some dock decorating going on."

As he came closer, I could smell his unwashed clothes, and the pungent wood chip and trout flesh odour from his fish smoker. I wanted to grab for the towel to cover my bathing suit, but I held his leering look and scowled. "What do you want, Mr. Grift?"

"Me? When have I ever wanted anything that I didn't already have?" Grift asked. "God's green earth creation at my disposal! I just came down to see if there was anything you wanted, Lainie? Anything at all?" He smacked his lips and scratched the hair at his base of his throat.

"I'm just fine, thank-you. You needn't trouble yourself," I answered.

"How long we been neighbours now, Lainie? Half a year? You've never paid me a visit."

"I work in town, Wally. I'm pretty busy."

"Oh yes . . . I can see that. But you didn't even come by to say thank-you to me for keeping your road cleared all winter. Your grandpa was a man of manners, Lainie. I figure he taught you better."

I stiffened, then sat up. "My grandpa built that road and saved you a bundle by allowing you to use it as access to your place. I know Grandpa maintained it in the summer, adding gravel, having the washouts graded. All you had to do was plow it in the winter. That was the deal, Mr. Grift."

"Well, I'm not saying it was, and I'm not saying it wasn't. But even if it was, your grandpa's dead now and there's nothin' on paper. You're the new owner, so I expect you to be paying me next winter to clear the road."

I shaded my eyes against the sun to see if Grift meant what he was saying. I responded, "Then I expect you won't be allowed access on my road."

Grift chuckled. "You been to some big university out on the coast, eh, Lainie?"

I stared at him.

"Don't they teach nothin' there? That road is what you now

call *public access*, because I been using it all these years and you can't deny me access to my own land. That's the law."

Wally Grift was the biggest bullshitter around, but I wasn't certain if he was correct or not. A cool breeze rippled off the lake, as I paused then said, "If that's the law, Wally, and that's the way you're going to be about it, then I'll find someone else with a snow blade to clear the road for me."

Grift grunted and spat into the water. "You're a little bit too feisty there, Lainie . . . just like your grandma. And you got her nice tight little ass. I remember when your grandparents moved in here, your dad about seven, your grandma no older than you are right now. She used to swim skinny at daybreak, right off this dock. I was barely old enough to shave, but I'd sit between the twin jack pines at my place and watch her nudey show from down the beach. Even though she'd had a kid pretty young, she still had a nice tight little ass, just like yours," he said, sneering.

I shot him a filthy look.

Grift licked his bottom lip where some of the spit still clung, "I'll just bet I could make your little ass squirm all over me."

I stood. "Get the hell off my dock!"

Grift didn't move, except to flick his fingers at my breast. "You got a nicer pair of hooters than your grandma did."

That's when Shale moved out from under the cedar, his hackles raised, a low growl rumbling in his throat. Grift ambled off the dock, making sure he didn't turn his back to Shale. "That dog's been shittin' in my yard since your grandpa rescued him from the pound," he said, extending his finger at Shale. "You'll be sorry if I catch that crappin' cur on my property again."

I never let Shale out loose without me after that, and I made sure he didn't forget his training. Last night, somehow, I left the patio screen unlatched and Shale took off after a raccoon or rabbit. I searched for him half the night, checked the highway over and over in case he'd been hit, even headed out in the motorboat around the point in the dark in case he'd swum off. I didn't suspect Grift until this morning, but he must have caught Shale immediately or else Shale would have come back when I first called him.

As I speed down the highway in the jeep with the windows wide open, the breeze whips my breath dry. There's a heat shimmer coming off the asphalt ahead. I feel if I could reach it, I'd evaporate. The iced cappuccino has curdled in my stomach. I need a plan to rescue Shale from Grift's shack. I am not good at plans. I have numerous ideas that I think are plans, but are merely fleeting desires. If I tell no one, the ideas careen into the ditch in my head, get stuck in a quagmire of procrastination. Other people sometimes come along and pull me out: Darrel and I had plans to tour Europe this year. If ideas escape my head before they fail, they become even more catastrophic. Europe is now like a derailment, evacuation pending a change in wind direction. If I could salvage my catastrophes, had a Red Cross relief plan, I'd be cycling Europe on my own, but I am here, speeding down the highway that leads out of Hematite, trying to rescue my inherited dog.

When I turn off the highway to the cabin, I expect to feel cooler air, a breeze coming off the lake; but even the birch and pine-shaded road ripples with stifling heat. My tires crunch down the gravel, a grasshopper leaps off into the underbrush, a crow caws at me for disturbing the afternoon stillness. When I reach the fork in the road, I spot Grift's truck parked out behind his ancient wood pile. He's beat me back. My guts clench when I think about Shale with a man who's made his livelihood from killing off wildlife. If wearing fur hadn't become politically incorrect, Wally Grift would be a rich man.

An earthy coolness rises from the crawl space when I lift the floorboards in the back bedroom closet. I see the three guns in their cases down there and wonder if they've been rusting in the dampness. I take out the .22. The bolt action sticks from being stored too long. I work it a few times, feel it loosen. I lift the pulpy cardboard flap of the ammo box. The thought of loading the gun makes my head feel as if I'm looking down from a thin-ledged height. The .22 bullets are a puny weight in my hand. I load several into the magazine and insert it into the stock. Breathe in; breathe out. I put the gun back in the crawl space and replace the floorboards. I will just stride over and ask for Shale; thank Grift for taking care of him for the night; pretend that Grift saved Shale from getting run over on the highway.

I start down the hallway and see a dark mass against the pine cupboards. Wally Grift is standing in my kitchen. I swallow my panic. The gun flashes into my head, but Grift turns at that moment and spots me where I stand.

"Well . . . home early today, Lainie?"

"What are you doing in my house?"

"Oh, I was passing by and saw the patio door open. Knowing you're normally at work at this time, I thought maybe you had a burglar. Lots of burglaries goin' on. You're not missing anything, are you Lainie?"

"I know you've got my dog, Grift."

"Your dog? Ha! I was referring to you missing other things— like maybe a nice bit of action."

"Where's Shale?" I demand.

"Oh, your dog's fine, Lainie. Tied up in my yard with a big chain."

"You son-of-a-bitch," I spit out.

"Getting feisty again? You are just like your grandma. She put up quite a fight right here in this same kitchen. Made it all the sweeter, Lainie. I like when a woman resists. The men and your pipsqueak dad off shooting ducks that afternoon."

My hand reaches out to the hallway wall to steady myself. "Get outta here, Grift, or I'll call the cops," I say, but I'm judging the distance to the door. I can outrun him if I can reach the door first.

He watches me eyeing the door and saunters across the room towards me, one of his arms twitching. "I guess your grandma liked it. She told them a big ol' bear barged into her kitchen. Imagine that . . . a big ol' bear."

The .22 is my only choice. I start to back towards the bedroom. I can't retrieve the gun before Grift stops me unless I'm able to slam the door shut and jam it long enough to pry the floorboards. Just as I'm prepared to bolt, there is a clatter. Shale, a large chunk of chain dragging behind, claws through the patio screen into the room. Before I can give the command, Shale clamps onto Grift's arm, hauling him down to the floor.

Grift is screaming as I pry the floorboards. When I point the gun at his head, he doesn't notice.

"Get your fuckin' dog off me," he bellows and tries to kick at Shale's head. Shale tightens his grip and yanks harder, dragging Grift in the opposite direction to prevent the kicks from connecting. A trail of blood smears across the kitchen floor.

"Shale, off!" I yell, the gun still lowered at Grift's head. Shale releases and crouches, growling and snapping, hackles raised, teeth bared.

Grift clutches his arm. "Your fuckin' dog's dead," he screams. "I'll have the police chief put a bullet in his brain." Grift stops yelling when he sees the barrel of the gun pointed at him.

"Maybe that should be *your* fate, Grift," I say.

He tries to stand and I rack the bolt. He slides back down.

It's another moment filled with the possibilities of derailment. From the corner of my eye, I see someone in the living room seated at the loom, weaving away her memories.

I aim high at the kitchen wall and pull the trigger. The sharp crack makes my ears ring. Shale doesn't flinch, the chain rattles behind him as he circles Grift, his teeth bared. Grift looks behind him at the small hole in the kitchen wall. A whimper—that I have to strain to hear over the ear-ringing—escapes him.

My fingers tremble as I aim the barrel at him, and say, "You drive yourself to the hospital, Grift, and when they ask you what happened as they're sewing your arm back together, you tell them a bear mauled you. You don't mention me or my dog. Because rape's a different story nowadays, and you won't like the ending. You got that, Grift? . . . A big ol' bear . . ."

Taking on Water

AS KAREN RUMMAGES THROUGH HER PURSE FOR THE CHEQUE book, Rod runs his wedding ring hand over the sleek white fibreglass hull. By the time she crosses the cramped 't' in Larter, Rod plunges his hands into his pockets, as if to hold in place the slight paunch around his middle that, in recent years, has come to indicate too much time spent behind a desk, a calculator, a computer screen. She watches him rock on the balls of his feet, another recent habit, one he normally reserves for corporate cocktail parties. Karen realizes that his focus has sailed right out of the showroom, onto another tack.

A few months earlier when the snow was giving way to slush, Rod said that he thought he would be happier if he had a new hobby to take his mind off things. The way he said *things* had turned their orthopaedic mattress into a bed of nails. She could choose to believe that *things* referred to the lingering illness and recent death of his mother, the three-day suspension of their twins for double-mooning the vice-principal, or the fact that his promotion to comptroller meant a much heavier workload. She

25

could choose to believe any or all of that, and she did. She hung onto her belief, but it didn't stop her from sliding out of their bed that night, wandering down to the kitchen, stretching across the cool linoleum in the pool of light from the open microwave door, regretting what she'd done.

The salesman helps winch the sailboat onto the trailer behind their van. Rod settles into the driver's seat and starts the van's motor. He argues on, as if he still has to convince Karen to buy the boat. "I'll be able to teach the boys to sail," he claims.

"The salesman said it's a two-man boat," she responds. "Doesn't that mean you can only take one passenger at a time?"

"It will be good for the twins to disconnect from each other a little. Neither of them even had a date for the prom," he states.

She says nothing, though it's the harder choice.

"Once they know how," Rod continues in the silence she leaves, "they can sail it together; maybe even start racing at the yacht club." He squints at the van's side mirrors, watching the boat hull glide out behind them, thirsty for water.

The idea of belonging to a yacht club makes Karen shudder. More water-worshippers. Despite this, an idea for a campaign strikes her and she pulls out her daytimer and makes a note to have one of the account executives in her office call the boat dealership and pitch advertising to them. She can see the magazine page—white sails against a backdrop of Lake Windigo evergreens, the caption: *Don't miss the boat*. Karen hadn't ever appreciated the resort- and cottage-dotted lake, unlike Rod, who had spent all the summers of his youth there. She didn't swim, feared water, irrationally sank to the bottom as soon as her feet could no longer touch. But she was savvy enough to recognize Lake Windigo's attraction. Rule number one of her personal advertising laws is *For eternity, people will seek the Garden of Eden*. If you can make them believe, with a picture and a few words, that a paradise is available to them, they will save their money and run up their credit cards to get it. She understands desire. It's a necessity of her job—writing words that stir people's longings. *Don't miss the boat!*

"Hmmm?" she says, realizing Rod asked a question.

"Did you bring the champagne?" he repeats.

"It's in the cooler," Karen replies.

"I thought the boys might get a kick out of christening the sailboat," Rod says.

Karen's forehead creases. "Is that what you wanted it for? How are we going to clean broken glass up off the beach? Whatever's left of the beach."

Rod's thumb drums on the steering wheel, a rapid war-dance beat. Karen watches his hand. The impatience of it matches the pulse in the vein next to her right eyebrow. The van's red speedometer needle creeps upwards as they gain highway speed. Her temple throbs. She notices for the first time that Rod's fingers have grown paunchy along with the rest of his body. He used to have long, narrow fingers, which made his hands look artistic. His hands were what first attracted her, the day she sat next to him in an economics lecture: the way his slender fingers wrapped loosely around his pen, as if they already knew about supply and demand and the spot between her shoulders that she liked to have stroked. She marvelled afterwards at the way love could anchor itself to such an obscure moment; an image burned into the heart. She looked up at his face that day. He smiled into his neatly trimmed beard and she fidgeted with her long straight hair to keep her hand from touching his mouth and freeing his smile. Now, all she sees are fat fingers, the flesh bulging around his wedding band.

Karen says, "The boys aren't joining us anyway. They decided to take extra hours when I told them we'd be spending the weekend getting the cottage back into some semblance of order."

"Why didn't anyone tell me?" Rod asks. "I'm going sailing, Karen. We can hire someone from the lodge next weekend to clean the place."

After a few moments of silence, he stops the van and gets out to ensure the bearings on the trailer aren't overheating. Karen knows she should roll down her window and call out, "Is everything all right?" Rod likes it when she does that. He likes reassuring her that he has things under control. She knows this in the same way she learned how he liked his steak cooked and for the same reason she once memorized all the lyrics to the Rolling Stones songs in Rod's album collection. She had wanted to please him, to be connected to him. She could start to do that again— nothing but a small courtesy is required. Instead, she turns her attention to the billowing white and grey cumulus columns that are invading the blue sky. Even though Rod rattles the safety chains and snaps the tie-downs to prolong his inspection, she ignores him. When they pull back onto the road, she watches the bands of sunlight and cloud-shadow emerge and recede on the uneven asphalt ahead of her. She disregards the scenic rock cuts, the evergreens and birches that line the highway. She makes herself restless thinking about the concrete texture of a cornerstone, a restaurant that serves spinach salad with raspberry vinaigrette, the glossy cover of an art catalogue, the way Mattheus undid his bow tie after a performance and slipped it out from the collar of his shirt. He was most demanding immediately following a performance. There were so few times he could just leave the concert hall without other commitments and join her. On those rare nights, her lies were elaborate but she considered them worth it.

As Rod turns into the cottage roadway, the smell of moist cedar reaches them. Karen braces herself for the worst. It's been two years since they've been here. Life has taken them away from the place: the boys started part-time jobs in the city, Rod's mother became too ill to be chauffeured out any longer, Rod took to golfing on the weekends, and Karen—she marvels at the thought—has had an affair.

Rod rolls down his window and breathes deeply. Karen aches from the unexpected familiarity of the place. The window frames are in need of paint, the trees taller, the underbrush shaggy, but essentially familiar. It strikes her as a cruel irony that this spot, this cottage, where she and Rod made love for the first time two decades earlier, could change so little in two years, while their marriage has been altered beyond recognition.

"I'm going to try backing right down to the water," Rod says. "It's more convenient if we don't have to use the public launch."

"Aren't you even coming into the cottage?" Karen asks, as she steps out of the van. "What if the place is full of mice?"

"Carving knives should still be in the left-hand drawer where my mother kept them."

Karen frowns. "You're not going to find me perched on a chair, screaming. I'm staying out here."

"Suit yourself." He calls this from the open van window as he starts to manoeuvre the trailer down the beach. The white hull of the boat is muscled towards the water. It reminds Karen of the underbelly of a shark. It reminds her of that first glimpse, two years ago, of Mattheus' taut, bare, white skin, smooth and dangerous. The trailing edge of the boat's dagger-board is like the crease of his tuxedo trousers, folded over the hotel chair back. Karen runs a few steps to catch up with the boat and then stands at the water's edge. As Rod slowly backs the trailer into the lake she puts her hand out and lets the hull glide past her fingers. She expects it to feel much colder.

"Look, Karen. If you're not going into the cottage, why don't you help me get the mast stepped?" Rod asks this as he discards his shoes and rolls up his pant legs. When he stands up, his face is flushed; but barefoot, there is a boyishness to him.

Karen eyes the long pole and has difficulty imagining Rod setting it upright into the boat on his own. She nods at him as a gust of wind off the lake puffs the skin on her arms into goosebumps. "Okay, but you're not really planning to take this out on the water today, right? It looks rough out there."

Rod stops untying the cords and looks at her. He talks easily most of the time: a man given to chatter rather than cogitation. But for the moment, there is only the calming sound of water washing sand and the wind's part in it. The pause makes Karen look out past him to the lake. When he does speak, she is doused with his words, as if they are whitecaps frothing over her. "I'm not certain, Karen, why it should matter to you . . . one way or the other . . . any more."

Her eyes dart back towards him, but his attention is already focused on the mast. He struggles to erect it: to line up the long pole—with its tendency to sway out of control so that he's forced to mimic a circus performer's balancing act—and sink it into the small hole. She does nothing to assist him, her arms limp at her side, the wind knocked out of her sails.

So, he does know. Maybe he's known all along. How did he find out? Those comments he made in the winter that she had chosen to interpret in an innocuous way—the ones that had coincided with the end of the affair—had he been trying to tell her that he knew? Why the hell hadn't he come out and said so? If he did know, how could he go on living as if it didn't matter? She fails to see that she's done the same—she has such a need to blame him.

The affair ended more abruptly than she'd expected. The new symphony board of directors found a replacement for the promotions director whom the old board had fired. They no longer needed an advertising agency; she no longer had an excuse to meet the conductor for executive lunches. Her final meeting with Mattheus was after a sold-out performance of Mozart. They had their own standing ovation in his apartment shower, the music still pulsing in their veins. She hasn't seen him since. She told herself everything happens for a reason, that she needed to renew her vows to Rod; but in her private darkness she watches Mattheus' expressive body bring the orchestra to crescendo, sees him shudder his release inside her, and she is conducting violin strings and flutes. She feels as guilty about her continued longing for him as she does about having slept with him.

With the wind coming off the lake in gusts, she wishes that Rod would start screaming questions. She wants to spill, wants to describe how when Mattheus made love to her, it was a complicated movement. She was a layout of white space and Mattheus the first exquisite mark on the page. She wants to hurt Rod further; wants justification for having hurt him at all. But for all Rod's words, he avoids talking about crucial things. Karen thinks for a moment that she'd settle for Rod chasing her with the ropes—the sheets he calls them—to try to strangle her, but instead he knots one, attaches it to the jib. The small sail flaps uselessly despite its gruff, whipping racket.

"The wind's pretty strong. Gusting too," Rod observes. "It's not directly onshore, though, so it shouldn't be too hard to take her out."

"You've never done this before, Rod. What are you talking about? There's that photo of you, when you were six, in the rubber dinghy with the piece of white sheet on a broom handle. That's the only sailing you've ever done!" How can he be so bloody oblivious to his own limitations? Why can't he absolve her of her guilt?

Rod tightens a wire shroud. "I spent a lot of time with the manuals and how-to books over the past year or two," he responds as he secures the boom in place, then floats the boat to dockside. He ties the boat there temporarily, then he tosses Karen a life jacket.

It's a challenge. Karen likes her water hot and in the bathtub and she knows that Rod knows it. Although for years he's tried to help her overcome her fear of drowning, he's been unsuccessful. When her feet no longer touch bottom, she panics, flails, sinks. Lake Windigo, with its water sports and cottage parties, with its bikini-peppered docks and lichen-armoured islands, has always threatened to swallow her.

Karen's fingers shake as she latches on the life jacket. She would panic watching him from the shore, anyway. She lowers herself into the sailboat without looking at her husband. Under her slight weight, the boat shifts and the boom swings across the deck. She ducks, imagines being in the middle of the lake and the boom banging her head, knocking her out and off the boat so that even the life jacket won't make a difference. She crouches at the back of the boat to stay out of the boom's way.

"You have to move up front. Run the jib," Rod insists, "otherwise you have to steer it."

She clambers to the front, crouching all the way. Rod boards and hoists the main sail. Its flapping racket makes her stomach clench. The wind gusts. The sun clouds over. Rod pushes them off the dock. There seems to be an interminable amount of time while he adjusts ropes, lowers the dagger-board, takes hold of the tiller. They are in a raging limbo. The boat rocks on the waves, inches its way backward towards the mound of rocks on the far side of the property line where the sandy part of the beach ends.

"Shift to the opposite side of the boat, Karen," Rod orders. "Pull in that end of the jib sheet. Not too tight. Just until the sail starts to resist."

The racket ceases as if someone has flicked a switch. The wind fills the sails; the craft darts past the side of the dock and angles towards the open water. Rod instructs Karen to lean back and the water streams past her backside in a chilling spray. The power of the vessel thrills Karen. No motor—just the potency of nature, the effectiveness of design. Rod trims the main sail, cleats the sheet. The boat surges ahead. When it's time to tack, he talks Karen through it: the moment to shift, the luffing of the sails, the retrimming, the resurgence. The craft heels through the water at a forty-five-degree angle. Karen braces her feet against the dagger-board trunk, her weight thrown back to counteract the force of wind in the sails. She can see the look of concentration on Rod's face as he holds the tiller steady and lends his weight to the cause. There's a moment of perfect balance as side by side, their stomach muscles quaking, they hold the boat there. The boat cuts so economically, the waves are sliced into submission.

The next moment a shifting gust catches them. The back of Karen's head dips into the water, her backside sits in it. Before she can attempt to pull herself back up, she is hurled forward as the sails careen down towards the lake on the opposite side. The inertia pitches her headlong towards them. Their stark whiteness looms in front of her, like a shroud about to encase her and drag her down to the bottom of the lake. She screams Rod's name.

He grabs the belt of her life jacket, as her hands flail in mid-air grasping for a hold. He hauls her back into the bottom of the boat, then lets out the main sail and struggles to steer the bow into the wind. The boat shudders upright again and bobs about directionless, abruptly impotent, the sails flapping and ineffectual.

Karen's tears mix with the water they have taken on, which sloshes around her backside and ankles. Rod is still perched on the gunwale. He shakes his head, relives the moment, a cockeyed grin of wonder on his face. Karen glances up at him, remembers when he used to look at her that way. Through her sniffles a laugh creaks out, rusty. It meets the wind, is carried across the lake. A loon surfaces near them. And then its mate.

"You okay?" he asks.

"Yeah," she replies.

Rod cautiously tightens the main sheet and steers the bow across the wind, takes control of the jib as well, while Karen hugs her knees at the bottom of the craft.

Rod looks down at her, smiles, "Wild ride, eh?"

"Yeah," she replies a second time.

The wind catches the sails again and pushes them forward on their new tack. Rod whoops. He tilts his head, looks straight up to the top of the mast, as if the answer might be there, and asks, "Do you still know all the Stones' lyrics to 'Sympathy for the Devil'? I can only remember the chorus."

Karen follows his gaze. The tiny flag atop the mast indicates the wind is maintaining a constant direction. She starts to sing the first verse, glancing at her husband, encouraging him to remember.

Rod nods and joins in as he steers them back towards shore.

Model Behaviour

"YOU'RE MAKING THE RIGHT CHOICE, JOHN. I'M COUNTING THE days myself."

John doesn't respond to the man in the navy suit—a Mr. Andrews from Human Resources—who is miming a golf swing, a long drive in the direction of the green cabinet. John's eyes dart to the padlock on it. He knows it's locked, but there's an illogical urge in him to get up and rattle it just to be sure.

Stacey (John forgets her last name), who arrived that afternoon with Mr. Andrews, shuffles more papers and indicates the last spot where John's signature is required. John peers through the bottom of his bifocals to see the x more clearly and can't help but be distracted by her pearly-white polished fingernails. Nails that length are useless for anything aside from pointing, or cat-scratching a man's back. He scrawls *John Nathan Hogarth* and hands Stacey back her pen.

He crosses his arms over his chest and leans back in his chair to make it look as if it's no big deal. The palm of his right hand is directly over his heart. It's pumping hard, circulating dread along with the oxygen. He wants to say to the two of them: The right choice, my ass. Early retirement package. Choose this or choose nothing.

It wasn't supposed to be like this. He imagined his retirement as a time when big honours would be bestowed on him. Hadn't he proved himself exemplary in the line of duty? What was the point of losing his sister Clare, and her son Danny—the only ones who mattered to him—otherwise?

His eyes dart to Mr. Andrews, who is crossing the room towards the green cabinet. John fights the urge to stand up. Mr. Andrews veers off to the window, and pointing south across the invisible line to the US, he says, "Yes, John. It's a different world out there. Terrorism, not smuggling, will be the focus for new recruits."

John snorts. "Now why would a terrorist cross the border here at Cranborough to come into Canada? They want access to the US. It's my neighbours in the building yonder that have to worry about terrorists."

Mr. Andrews exchanges a look with Stacey. John can tell that they're satisfied to have purged another old geezer off the payroll. They have no idea what the field threats are, coming out of their headquarters office and spewing world politics.

John can't resist; he wants to be an old cuss. "Anyone that wants in bad enough will just wait until after midnight, anyway." He knows these two had nothing to do with the cutbacks a few years earlier that reduced the Cranborough crossing from a twenty-four- to an eighteen-hour facility, but he's willing to take it out on them. He used to love night shifts. The truckers; the odd family driving all night on vacation, making time while the kids slept in the back; the teenagers coming back late from dances across the line on weekends. They all needed to be detained once in a while for their own good. Wake them up, sober them up, make them fit for the road again, some hot coffee while he searched their vehicles. And once in a while, bingo! He'd come up with liquor stashed in the spare tire compartment or notice, under the harsh office lights, that the vacationing woman was likely wearing several brassieres on top of each other. Nothing earth-shattering. But it was important to let people know they couldn't get away with anything, not while John Hogarth was at the window.

Mr. Andrews responds to his comment. "That's why they put in the state-of-the-art surveillance technology here, John. If undesirables get across, we've got a picture of them doing it."

John has to smile at that. "Maybe you could teach those cameras to shoot out their tires, too," he challenges and laughs at his own sarcasm.

"Mr. Hogarth, I reviewed your work records. There was nothing about you ever shooting out someone's tires." Stacey says this with a coy voice, trying to cajole him, relieve the tension.

John feels his face redden. She's got the better of him. He rubs his hand over his forehead, feels what's left of his hairline.

Shoving the last of the documents into the briefcase, Stacey smiles at him and says, "You'll have a million details to clear up in these last few days, so we shouldn't take up any more of your day, Mr. Hogarth."

Mr. Andrews extends his hand. "Good luck, John."

And it's over. The rest of his life leaves in a briefcase for some file drawer in the city. John goes through the motions of the rest of his shift. At 11:30 p.m., he tells Munroe, the newest man at the crossing, to go home early to his wife.

"I'll lock up," he tells him. "It's been a quiet one. I've got a few things to start packing up here anyway."

John sees that Munroe gets into his car. He stands outside the back door of the building, watching the moths and mosquitoes swarm the floodlights; the mosquitoes mistaking the heat for fleshly warmth; the moths, unable to navigate without the moon in front of them, flying round and round in false worship. He takes a deep breath. On the August air there is the unmistakable damp taste of heavy dew and the onset of autumn. He thinks of his sister, Clare. Wonders how she's making out with the harvest. Feels guilty for the millionth time. Not for pursuing the charges against his nephew, Danny; but because he can't be there, helping

Clare out. Can't fulfil his duty to his sister, his promise to be there for her after Luke's tragic death. He wonders how much strength it would take to rip the screen door off the side of the building. But even that is just a fleeting thought. His last brave action was putting Danny behind bars. There's been an impotency to his actions ever since; a need to second-guess himself that never existed before. He has to take action now. He has to empty the green cabinet.

From the trunk of his car he removes the cardboard boxes in which the carry-out boys at the Co-op have packed his groceries for the past few weeks. He's saved up newspapers too. He heads back inside.

As he swings the doors to the green cabinet open, John exhales with a quiet relief. In the past few years he has often feared that someone would open the cabinet without his knowledge and discover its contents. But there they all stand, their specific placement undisturbed; rows of them, precisely assembled, painted with attention to detail. Each of them completed between the hours of midnight and 6:00 a.m., ever since the Cranborough border crossing started to close at midnight. John found it easier to stay there after his evening shift, rather than go home to the midnight flicker of old movies on the television set.

His eyes dart first to his favourites, all on the top shelf: the Mercedes coupe, the Bentley sedan, the Rolls-Royce—solid, massive, dependable automobiles with impeccable moral standards. His back straightens a little whenever he picks one of them up. He likes the way the chrome dominates the front of them; the way they exude authority when you view them head-on. His stomach cramps when he looks at the '60s muscle cars—those were Danny's favourites—Cougars, Firebirds, Mustangs, Super Bees. Cars that John knew intimately, taught Danny about. Car talk became the mutual, safe place in the months after Danny was left fatherless at age six. John bought him his first model, helped him assemble it over two or three nights: a dragster, its long nose and pivoting axles delighted Danny. Over the newsprint-covered table and airplane-glue-laden toothpicks, they'd keep up a steady stream of chatter.

"So, what came through last night, Uncle John?"

"Oh, you missed a beauty, young fella! A Plymouth GTX hard-top." John would wait for Danny's elfish face to be dutifully impressed before he'd continue. "Brand-spankin' new '69 with a 426 Hemi. Prettiest deep blue and the chrome on fire in the sunset. Newlyweds driving up from Montana . . . just kids . . . still wet behind the ears."

"Whoa, I wish I'd seen it!"

"Yep."

"Did they have anything illegal on them?"

John snorted, "Such as what?"

"I don't know, like gangster guns or something."

"I said they were newlyweds, didn't I?"

"Yeah, but like Bonnie and Clyde or something? They could outrun the cops in a car like that. They could outrun you, Uncle John."

"Where'd you get the idea some punk could outrun your uncle?" John would knuckle-rub Danny's scalp until he'd squeal with giggles, then they'd settle back to work, gluing tiny bits of plastic together to make a chassis, decorating the finished exterior with shiny decals and paint. Clare would come in with moist heavy cakes and milk, the strain of being widowed, with three boys to raise, etched into her features.

She'd say, "It's late, Danny. You have to get ready for bed."

"Ah Mom, why can't I stay up like Ralph and Mack?"

"They've got chores still. They're older," she'd reply and her vocal chords would sound as if they were being stretched in a wringer washer.

"I'll make sure he gets to bed, Clare," John would say. "We'll only be a few minutes more."

Had his own indulgence turned his nephew bad? What if he'd said, "Do as your mother says, Danny!" Would things have turned out differently?

John rubs his gut. How many hours since he's eaten? He could still get to the diner before it closes. Cheap buggers on their headquarters expense accounts never even offered to spring for a sandwich out! He picks up several pieces of newspaper, balls them up, shoves them into the bottom of the first box. Using both hands, he reaches up for the Thunderbird, places it on a flat sheet of paper, starts to wrap, turning the car as he goes, side over side, like a roll-over in the ditch. He puts the Thunderbird in the box and takes down the LeSabre. By the time he seals the first cardboard flaps, a shelf in the green cabinet stands empty. His hands are black from the newsprint. He stands looking at them, palms up, compliant. He could beg forgiveness with soiled hands. He never did. He went to Clare after Danny's arrest, but it was to explain to her why he had no choice but to turn Danny in for cigarette smuggling, to defend his own actions, make her see his side.

"I gave him a chance, Clare. Something I've never done for anyone before. I told him I knew, that he had to stop. He thought I didn't have the guts to see my warning through." John had said these words that November morning, standing outside her kitchen door, staring at the thick skim of ice on the rain barrel's surface, rather than witness the hatred in her eyes.

Her voice sounded like pot scrubbers on aluminum as she dredged up words from the root cellar of her soul: "John Nathan, you are a filthy disgrace. You'd see your nephew rot in jail for the sake of some lousy cheap cigarettes. That's a despicable crime against your own family—far worse than what Danny did. Why the hell don't you look for the sick hoodlums that smuggle the drugs? Maybe Danny's life would be different if you'd kept the goddamn drugs out of this town."

He hadn't set foot in Clare's yard since, even though Danny only served a three-month sentence. Danny was back in the Cranborough Hotel playing the tough ex-con, talking about the hardships and bullshit of jail, drifting sporadically into the city to work in some garage, and back out when he was down on his luck, staying long enough to help Ralph and Mack with part of a harvest or with some calving. John had to avoid running into him, into any of them. Working evenings was a good way to do that, because that's when Danny would prowl the town. Sleeping in the daytime kept John out of Clare's way. Many times he'd contemplated accepting a transfer, but in the end he always rejected it. *Don't run from having done the right thing, John*, he'd lecture himself; but never far from his thoughts was some scheme for redeeming himself, worming his way back in. Schemes he never managed to act upon. He couldn't help but think that they needed to see the error in their ways and come to him; after all, hadn't he let his own life slip by while he dedicated himself to being there for them? Once, he even wrote a letter to Ann Landers seeking advice, but he never mailed it, afraid of her answer.

John looks at the clock in his office. It's midnight. He steps out the office door, carrying the flare-orange pylons, placing them in a line. The mighty barrier. Canadians have actually turned around at the pylon line and paid American dollars for a hotel room. He shakes his head. As if this could stop anybody but a too-polite Canadian. Most people who are bent on crossing don't even bother knocking them over or moving them out of the way; they drive around the "entering US Customs" side and chance a head-on collision. Of course, there's never anyone coming from the other side, because the border is supposed to be closed. The camera has recorded all this, he imagines. He's never looked at the tapes. That's the day shift's job, but he's witnessed it directly, while he's stayed after midnight piecing his model cars together. On occasion, he's been tempted to walk out and scare the hell out of whoever was sneaking through, but he wasn't supposed to be there. Same as them. Now, he looks down the highway towards the US. There are no oncoming headlights. No latecomers. No one's been through for the past half hour. Quiet. In all those years, why hadn't he made a major drug bust? Had he not been looking hard enough? Maybe no dealers would dare cross on the shift that John Nathan Hogarth worked. *He's the guy who put away his own nephew.*

He hankers to stop packing up the cars and work on an unfinished model. A Dodge Viper. Damnedest thing on wheels. The urge is like a burning in his gut. Maybe he's addicted to the glue, or else why would it matter so much? Why does Clare's forgiveness matter so much? Retirement stretches ahead of him like the highway out of his country. He goes back into the building, hangs the "Canada Customs Closed" sign in the window, and shuts off all the interior lights with the exception of his desk lamp.

He denies himself the pleasure of the Viper, and starts to wrap the z28 from the second shelf. He has two boxes sealed and is scrunching up newspaper to start wrapping the trucks from the fourth shelf when the sound of the first shot echoes through the office. At first John is puzzled by the sound. The second shot is followed by crashing glass and John realizes it's gunfire. He ducks behind his desk, still clutching a Chevy short-box. He realizes that the exterior lights are no longer on; probably the camera has been shot out as well. He hadn't noticed a vehicle approaching—they must have come up with their headlights switched off. He is on his knees, his mind racing. Only someone with major cargo would be going to such lengths. Drug runners. He needs to tail them at a safe distance, call the RCMP detachment for back-up, and have them arrested. He should follow them in his own Lincoln so they don't suspect. The keys are in his pocket. For a split second, he imagines the accolades, he sees Clare's face when she reads the local paper, then he hears the motor revving as the culprits speed away. He has to act quickly. Crouched behind the desk, he remains on his knees, his hands clasped in front of him for a long time after the sound of their motor is just a memory.

What Jeanie and Ella Canned

FOR ALMOST TWENTY YEARS THEY HAD DONE THEIR CANNING together: peas, carrots, beans, beets and dill pickles in quart jars; mustard pickles and relish in pints. Whenever the raspberries were abundant and not too wormy they'd can them too and eat them with cream and white bread during the winter. Both their families loved their cooking. Both their husbands squabbled over how much garlic should be in the dill pickles. So when the tire that Walt was removing from the split rim launched into the air as if it were a missile, spattering Walt against the concrete wall of the garage that bore his name, it was natural that Ella should be the first one at Jeanie's side. It was fitting that Ella's ample soft shoulders should absorb the tears from Jeanie's sunken eyes. It was assumed that Ella should organize the church women into making perogies and cabbage rolls by the hundreds for the sit-down dinner after the funeral. It was expected that Ella would be the one to ensure all the leftover salads, casseroles and baking were covered with plastic wrap when she left Jeanie's house in the September dusk of the day they buried Walt. And so it seemed natural that the friendship of Jeanie and

Ella should wind together more tightly—like a wheat weaving, like the braid on a *kolach* bread—in the face of such a tragedy.

But that was not to be.

It was getting close to Christmas. That's when things started to unravel.

"Jeanie, I'm going downtown. You need anything?" Ella phoned while her car warmed up in the driveway.

"What could I need?" Jeanie snapped. The morning mail had just arrived. Still no insurance settlement, and the gas company was sending her a bill with Overdue stamped in red across it.

"Family Fare's got mushroom soup, three for a dollar," Ella coaxed.

"I got lots."

"I'll pick you up some."

"I got lots."

"You want to come with me tomorrow? Saan store's got towels on special—those little Christmas finger towels," Ella said, the receiver pressed to her ear as she peered down at the snow melting off her boots onto her kitchen linoleum.

Jeanie answered, "I don't think I need towels. I've got enough towels to last me now."

"But for gifts?" Ella suggested and then wished she hadn't when the line hummed its silence. "Okay, then I'll call you later," she added. She hung up the phone and bending down on one knee she took a tissue from her winter coat pocket and wiped up the puddled water. When she stood up, her cheeks were flushed red from the exertion.

After shopping, Ella dropped by Jeanie's house. "Oh, the stores are already so busy! I need a cup of coffee." She stamped her boots on Jeanie's back step which hadn't been shovelled and was a mix of packed and fresh snow. Jeanie was still wearing the hair net she slept in.

Ella noticed that Jeanie's turquoise blouse hung on her the way a garden scarecrow hangs on a stick frame. She used to be jealous of the way Jeanie could eat and eat and not gain weight, while she just had to look at the sour cream for her waist to expand. But since Walt's death, Jeanie had become even thinner and Ella felt bloated with pity whenever she sat down in her friend's tidy yellow kitchen.

As she stirred double cream into her coffee, Ella asked, "You want me to give you a perm before Christmas?"

Jeanie reached up to her hair, discovered the hair net and pulled it off. "No, I'm only going to church. I'll wear my hat."

"Oh that reminds me. Clifford wanted to get tickets for St. Ivan's hall. He says he's buying you one. You're coming with us." Ella blurted it out. She'd been wondering for days how to bring it up. They hadn't missed a St. Ivan's New Year's dance in over a dozen years, not even the year Clifford was getting over pneumonia. Walt had always bought the tickets; Ella had arranged for a shared babysitter when the kids still needed one.

Jeanie looked at Ella. She sucked in her breath and her beaklike nose narrowed around the nostrils. "Clifford crazy or what?" she demanded.

Complaining about their husbands had filled many a jar over the years, but there had always been unspoken rules, the central one being: if one of them complained about her husband, the other was permitted to sympathize and then complain about her own husband. There was no complaining about the other's husband allowed. With Walt dead and buried, Jeanie had no husband to complain about, and Ella had no stomach for complaining to Jeanie about Clifford any more. The result was like changing the steps to the polka, so when Jeanie called Clifford crazy, Ella felt an enormous relief, as if she were light on her feet again: they could now complain about the same husband. Ella did what she did best and laughed, then added, "I've been telling you for years, Clifford's a crazy old coot! And you know how stubborn! He won't take no for an answer. You'll have to come."

Jeanie hesitated. Her mouth looked as if it might break into one of her crooked smiles, but then she pursed her lips and stated through her teeth, "I'm not going to no New Year's dance without a husband. Am I supposed to dance on Walt's grave?"

Ella searched her coffee cup for a response. There was only

the cream-whitened brew and the green geometric pattern on the cup's rim. No answers. Ella remembered the years when Jeanie had been furious at Walt's habit of working extra late at his garage, then expecting a hot supper on the table when he got home. Jeanie would get out of bed and reheat it for him; the meat dried out, the vegetables soggy. Sometimes Walt would bring a customer home with him: one of the farmers from the surrounding area who could pay cash for new truck parts after selling some of his herd. They would eat Jeanie's midnight supper, sit around until 3:00 a.m. polishing off a bottle of rye. First thing in the morning Jeanie would phone. "Ella," she would say, "remind me to dance on his grave when he kicks the bucket."

The worst always blew over. Neither of them had ever imagined their words blowing up in their faces.

Ella clutched the steering wheel tightly as she manoeuvred over the icy roads home. She told Clifford in bed that night that Jeanie had refused to come to the dance.

"I'll have a talk with her," Clifford said. "She can't stay home and wither up."

Ella asked, "You don't think this is maybe rushing her?"

"Walt was a good man, but Jeanie didn't have it so easy with him all the time. Now he's gone and Jeanie is still a good-lookin' woman. She needs to get out of the house," he answered and pushed Ella's flannel nightie up her thigh. He rubbed his greying moustache into the fleshy folds of her neck and she didn't mind much. Sex, which she often lacked enthusiasm for, empowered her that night. What she had secretly imagined would be the one bright spot for her friend—not having to put up with Walt's demands in bed any longer—now made Ella pity Jeanie even more. Poor Jeanie, alone. When Clifford gave his final thrust inside her, Ella felt as if she'd won a blue ribbon prize and she said a prayer of thanks that her husband was alive to keep his side of the bed warm.

The next day after work, Clifford came in the back door whistling.

"How come you're late?" Ella asked, the wooden spoon in her hand pointed towards him.

"I stopped by Jeanie's," he replied. "The foreman bought everyone a Christmas ham. I thought Jeanie could use it more than us. Anyway, it's fixed up. She's coming to St. Ivan's."

"Well," Ella said and the spoon drooped in her hand. "That's good then."

As he unlaced his work boots, Clifford asked, "Were you over there to see the stove?"

"What stove?"

"The kids bought Jeanie a stove for Christmas. It was delivered early."

"A stove?" The word gushed out of her as if it were scalding coffee.

"Yeah, one of those deals with the solid elements, self-cleaning oven, the whole works!"

"Where'd they get the money for that? I thought Mickey was laid off as of January."

"Well, I guess they found the money or used credit. Something to cheer their mother up," Clifford answered.

Ella sat down to eat and fiddled with her fork. She wasn't upset because her own three kids had good jobs yet failed to buy her expensive gifts. Her agitation stemmed from not being the first person to hear the news about the stove. She glanced up at the phone on the kitchen wall and wondered why it hadn't rung. She pushed her plate away, the food half-eaten. That night in bed, she thought about Jeanie, the new stove, the meatballs and mashed potatoes she had scraped off her plate into the garbage. Her body rumbled its emptiness under the electric blanket.

Jeanie arrived the next morning with offerings to fill it up. "Such an even heat in the oven like I've never had," she explained to Ella as she passed her the plate of thumbprint cookies for the fourth time. "And the timer is easy to use, too."

Ella turned each cookie bottom up before she took a bite. After the seventh cookie was inspected and she still hadn't found one overdone, she asked, "So, why didn't you tell me you were getting a new stove?"

"Who knew?" Jeanie answered. "It was the kids' idea."

"You knew yesterday."

Jeanie frowned. "Well, Clifford dropped in. Didn't he tell you?" Jeanie asked, then added, "He had some of my butter buns. He doesn't take no for an answer, just like you said." Jeanie lowered her sharp chin towards her shoulder, as her eyebrows shot up. It was the pose she used to strike whenever Walt told a dirty joke. It expressed her initial disapproval so she was free to laugh at the punch line.

Ella didn't find anything amusing. She reached for her eighth thumbprint cookie. The maraschino cherry glistened, an artificial red. Her lip curled back as she nibbled it off the top.

For Christmas, Ella bought Jeanie her favourite Avon perfume in a holiday decanter. Jeanie gave Ella two new releases of *Company's Coming* cookbooks. On the surface it appeared like any other Christmas except that Jeanie stopped short of fully participating and took up reminiscing. Ella was getting tired of hearing about all of the wonderful Christmases Jeanie had spent with Walt. The years he took Mickey and Babs to chop down a Christmas tree in the bush (the kids came home half-frozen and crying, Ella wanted to remind Jeanie). The year he surprised her with two plane tickets to Las Vegas (she was terrified of flying). The year he bought twin snowmobiles (never mind that Jeanie had cursed the machines and refused to join the Sno-go club when Walt was still alive). Walt's death had purified Jeanie's love for him.

Over turkey leftovers on Boxing Day, Ella said to Clifford, "It's as if she's making home-brew out of Walt."

"What?" Clifford exclaimed as he spooned out dollops of cranberry jelly onto his plate.

"Yeah, she's taking the mash and distilling it into 180 proof. And same result too—she's gone blind from it! Blind to every fault Walt ever had."

"Now Ella," Clifford chided, "what kind of talk is that? You're her friend. If you think she's dwelling on the past, help her think about something new!"

Ella folded a perogy into her mouth and chewed silently. She phoned over after the dishes were done. "Jeanie," she said, "Pascala's got a boxing week sale on. Let's go see if we can find new dresses for New Year's!"

At the store Jeanie insisted on something black. "I can't be wearing hot pink and Walt buried just these three months."

Ella chose a red frock which made her body appear stouter and her complexion ruddier, but it wasn't until she saw Jeanie model her choice that she blushed crimson. Jeanie's dress was a sombre black, but had a large diamond-shaped cut-out over the bosom. She had little cleavage left to show, but the dress revealed all of it.

"Walt would have divorced me if I'd brought home a dress like this," Jeanie trilled.

"Go ahead, buy it!" Ella assured her. "Out with the old, in with the new!"

With their purchases next to them in the car, Ella complained about how she wished Clifford would go back to work already: he was driving her crazy over the holidays. She ignored the look in Jeanie's eyes that said, *At least you have a husband.* Ella finished with that and bragged about Clifford's Christmas bonus, big enough to pay for her new dress and maybe new wallpaper for the kitchen and bathroom too. "I'm glad he doesn't have his own business. At this time of the year you need a steady paycheque." Ella couldn't stop the words, couldn't stop thinking about the fact that Jeanie could buy a dress with a cut-out that begged to play peek-a-boo with a man.

By the time they arrived at the dance on New Year's Eve, St. Ivan's hall was crowded. Streamers and balloons hung from the ceiling rafters. A metallic Happy New Year sign was strung across the stage over the heads of the band members. Jeanie had protested about getting to the dance too early. She didn't want to see the swivelling heads and nudging elbows when she arrived. She insisted, "Better to get there when the place is packed, then nobody notices you come in." Because of this, they didn't get their usual table at the back of the hall. Ella had to wedge herself into a seat next to the wall with the band amplifiers blasting into her ears. She covered them and shook her head, but Jeanie laughed as if her friend was a big kidder.

"I'll get some drinks," Clifford shouted and disappeared into the crowd. Returning with three glasses, he shouted, "Bottoms up!"

Jeanie swigged her gin and tonic and smacked her lips. Ella nursed hers and was careful that their first dance was a butterfly, so that Jeanie wouldn't be left alone at the table. It was too soon after for Jeanie to be dancing, but Clifford waved his hand in the air as if he were swatting flies; he wouldn't take no for an answer. After that, every husband and a few bachelors at St. Ivan's hall took it as their personal mission to ensure that the widow Lestowicki didn't sit one out. When no one else asked, Clifford took her up. He was left with the waltzes. Ella counted down New Year's Eve by ticking off the seconds of Jeanie and Clifford's Happy New Year's kiss. It was one second too long and Ella could feel the irregular rhythm of her heartbeat, out of sync with "Auld Lang Syne."

A few minutes later in the smorg line, Ella looked over at Jeanie's overloaded plate. "All that won't be good for your heartburn at this hour," she said and laughed, because it was still what she did best.

"I know," Jeanie answered, her face flushed, "but I'm so hungry from all the dancing."

At the table, the elastic from Ella's party hat was cutting into her neck. She looked around to see others still wearing theirs. She sighed in resignation, wiped her chin with her party napkin and said to Jeanie, "You must be tired. We'll take you home after this."

Jeanie nodded and said, "We'll go, but I'm not tired. I've already asked some people over. Clifford said you'd stay. I asked Bulnowchucks, Martizinskis, Nester and Bill Bozuk too. They all sent such nice flowers when Walt died."

Jeanie's yellow kitchen was hard on the eyes after the dim lighting and smoke of St. Ivan's hall. Along with coffee, Jeanie served a bottle of Walt's rye from out of the back of the cupboard, and platters full of dainties and cookies from her freezer. She reapplied her lipstick and touched up her hair. While the Bozuk brothers played the spoons, she sang along with the others.

Later, when the brothers started a few yodelling numbers, Ella decided to go check on why Jeanie was taking so long bringing her a drink. Ella left the yodellers in the living room and found Jeanie, in the kitchen, crying in the circle of Clifford's arms, the peek-a-boo cut-out of her dress pressed up against his chest. Clifford's hands startled up from their nesting place on her buttocks.

"What the hell is this?" Ella spluttered, her own hands starting to shake, despite the fact she clamped them together in front of her as if she were praying.

Jeanie tried to twirl around, but Clifford held her by the arms, looked over the top of her head at his wife. "She's having a hard time, Ella. Can't you see that?"

"No, as a matter of fact, I can't see that," she hissed. "I didn't bring my glasses tonight."

Jeanie pulled away and wiped her eyes with the heels of each hand. "Ella . . . Ella, I was just thinking about all the years . . . and Walt. Don't misunderstand." Jeanie laughed, but she had never laughed as easily as Ella and it came out thin and watery.

Ella answered, "I'm going to get our coats, Clifford."

"Oh Ella, don't be so pig-headed," Jeanie snapped.

With her coat on, Ella stood in the kitchen, the room swaying around her, waiting for Clifford to pull his boots on at the back door. Jeanie had disappeared into the bathroom. The spoon-playing and yodelling continued in the living room.

Clifford said to his wife, "Wait there. I'll start the car, let it warm up."

"I'll come now."

"You say good-night to Jeanie," he growled and went out the door.

Ella looked around the kitchen for an indication of how a friendship grows from infancy to old age. The room was its usual neat and tidy self. It provided no answers.

On the counter sat one of Ella's own Tupperware containers

which Jeanie had borrowed and not yet returned. Ella picked it up, sniffed, then tasted the crumbs at the bottom. Matrimonial squares, she decided. She snapped on the lid, then placed the container on the large, front, element of Jeanie's new stove. She turned the knob to low—just enough heat to melt without over-cooking—and headed out the door.

As she eased into the car, Clifford, his bare hands wrapped around the frigid steering wheel, asked, "Did you talk to Jeanie?"

"Oh for sure, I did," Ella replied and her puff of breath frosted up the passenger window. "We decided what we would can this year."

Too Much Beauty ... Is Curse

"YOU HAVE TO BELIEVE IF YOU VANT ME TO HELP YOU," BABA SAID
to me, as she wiped the beef gravy off the plates with bits of bread
crusts, adding them to the bacon rinds for the dogs' evening
meal.

"I do believe, Baba," I responded and picked up the last dirty
spoon from the table.

She didn't look up, but I sensed her watery blue eyes could see
me. "Don't waste it food, Anna," she said, sweeping the crumbs
off the checkered oil cloth onto the heap.

"No Baba," I answered. I reached for a bread crust and quickly
wiped the smear of sour cream off the spoon.

"Take outside," she said, handing me the plate of scraps. She
looked at my face; focused on my cheek; narrowed her eyes at the
mole. Baba was the only person who could stare at the mole and
not shudder. Sometimes I tried to imagine how ugly the *Old
Country* must have been, if Baba could look at my face without
flinching. I envisioned a hovel covered in drizzle and chimney
soot, a stack of rotting hay. I decided, in my twelve-year-old

mind, that there were no blue skies, no golden wheat fields in the *Old Country*. I figured that's why Baba and other Ukrainians immigrated to Manitoba: they were searching for colours. They needed rich hues—not just traditional red and black—for the icons on the walls and banners of the church.

The sound of the back door brought the dogs running. They nuzzled the bowls as I tried to fill them, food falling on their heads as they scrambled for every morsel. I was careful to divide the rations exactly in half even though I preferred the collie, Fannie, over Duke the mutt, and would gladly have slipped her more except that I suspected Baba would consider that a sin. I couldn't risk that.

Baba said I had to believe in order for her to help me. I wanted to believe. I knew she meant I must believe in the Bible and Jesus, but what I wanted to believe in mostly were miracles. Since the Bible was filled with miracles—loaves and fishes, parting seas, healed lepers—I reasoned that everything should be fine. I left the plate on the steps and walked out to the edge of the ditch. The smell of damp earth emerging from the snow was enough to make my chest feel full, ready to burst with possibility. As the grey hushed dusk settled onto the farmyard, I stood in the ditch wearing Baba's oversize galoshes, pushing the length of the boots into the mud. The wet gumbo oozed up around the rubber sides. I lifted the boots, first one then the other. The mud sucked at the soles. I loved the feel of that crucial balance, when the suck of the mud and the pull of my foot were of equal force; that feeling that if I were to tug just a little too hard, the mud would suck harder too, until it won; my foot flying out, me flailing, bootless. I was striving for that balance with the mud for so long that the last of the dusk light vanished and my feet grew cold; yet I didn't stop. I couldn't help myself. It was as if I would always be attracted to the wonder of dark and unbecoming things.

"Anna! Come dry dishes," my mom called from Baba's back door. "I have to go help Aunt Sophie clean the church before the blessing of the baskets."

The mud squelched as I pulled out. I trudged towards the

peeling white of the clapboard farmhouse, looking backwards in the ice crystal snow to see the stained trail behind me. I walked an extra circle cleaning the sides of the boots carefully, so Baba would have no complaint about the mess. Each Easter she scrubbed every surface of her house—the smell of Pine-Sol and paste wax as prevalent as that of cabbage and garlic in her kitchen—and heaven help anyone who dirtied it. When Gedo was still alive, he changed his socks in the cellar before he walked on Baba's Easter floors.

"Go vash your hands," Baba said. "Then, you vipe for me." She pointed to the flour sack tea towels on a wall hook.

I was headed towards the small bathroom when I heard my mom start: "Mama," she said to Baba. "You really should think about selling some of your eggs. You should see now in the city— they set up a booth in the mall—you should see the prices they charge for them."

"I don't make pysanka to sell them," Baba chastised as if Mom had sworn.

I knew they'd be at it for a few minutes, so I bypassed the bathroom and went to the small corner bedroom where I slept when I visited Baba. I pushed aside the curtain that served as a door and straightened it shut behind me. From under the clothes in my suitcase, I pulled out a square pink stationery envelope. Its flap was worn from being tucked and untucked so often. On the front I'd written *Fortunes* in fancy script. I dumped the contents. Little strips of paper, pale green and white, littered the paisley quilt.

I chose one. It read: "*Self-knowledge is the key to understanding.*" And another: "*Your kind nature endears you to many.*" And others: "*Shrewd thinking will lead you down the road to success. You will win success in whatever you adopt. Beware the folly of pride.*"

On Friday nights Mom allowed me to go to the Chinese restaurant in town with my friend Suzie for a Coke and an egg roll. Mom was always saying that it was important for me to get out and have some fun. She'd say that with this weird little quiver in her throat, the same sound she made when she talked about my dad taking off when she was pregnant with me. It was good to escape the house then, because even though I'd start out happy about Mom feeling sorry for me, I'd end up resenting it. Going out also kept me from thinking bad thoughts about my dad: I couldn't decide if he really left when Mom was pregnant, causing her to be full of poisonous hate that turned into a mole on my face while I grew inside her; or if he actually left the day I was born, after seeing my face through the hospital nursery window for the first time. Either way, it seemed safer to blame an absentee dad for my affliction than to accuse an omniscient God.

Mr. Woo at the Chinese restaurant gave Suzie and me free fortune cookies because we never made any trouble like some of the kids in town. A gang of boys we knew used to call Mr. Woo a *chink* and pull their eyes aslant when he told them—in singsong English, arms waving in the air like a conductor's—to take their feet off the chairs. While those boys were being difficult, I stared down at the plum sauce congealing on my plate while Suzie, her mouth agape, watched the commotion through her thick glasses, pushing them up her nose so she wouldn't miss anything. I felt ashamed of those boys. I liked Mr. Woo's wide grin. I always smiled back. Though even Mr. Woo averted his eyes after glancing at me.

Suzie told me once that she heard you had to eat not just the cookie, but the fortune too, if you wanted the fortune to come true. Soon afterward, I got one that read: "*A serious man will fall in love with your laugh.*" When I returned home that night, I opened my curtains to the moon and stars, kneeled down on my bed and swallowed the tiny slip with a drink of milk.

Baba's voice called from the kitchen, startling me from my daydream. "Anna, vat you doing?"

"I'm coming, Baba."

I scooted to the tiny bathroom and scrubbed my hands. Reaching for the towel, I tried to avoid looking in the mirror over the sink, but once I caught sight of the mole I couldn't stop myself from touching it. My damp fingers grazed over its pocked and ridged surface. I could feel the hard bristle tip of the single hair that grew from it, which Mom encouraged me to trim off as soon as the hair became visible.

"No use making it more obvious," Mom often said, giving me a hug. She hugged me whenever we talked about the mole. I liked the hugs, but I knew she would never kiss that cheek. The *birthmark*, Mom called it. Never the lesion or blemish or, more accurately, the mole. *Birthmark* put it in the realm of skin blotches that were there from birth, but which sometimes disappeared of their own accord. My *birthmark* was there from birth but had done anything but disappear. It had grown proportionately with me, so that it continued to obliterate more than a third of my left cheek and erupted like a small volcano off the plateau of my cheek bone. If I turned my head away from the mirror at just the right angle and peered out of the corner of my eyes, I could make my nose disappear behind the mole. Once, a year earlier, I took a razor blade to the very edge of it, thinking I could just shave it off; that underneath, the skin would be peaches and cream. The mole bled for almost an hour. Mom said another five minutes and we would have had to go for a suture to the hospital. The scab fell off weeks later and there was an extra lump left behind.

When I finally came into the kitchen, Baba was at the sink. She reached around her puffed-wheat body and plunged her hands into the scalding dishwater. "Too much beauty," she said, "is curse."

She knew I had been looking in the mirror again.

"I know, Baba," I whined. "I'm not asking to be beautiful. It's a worse curse to have this on my face!"

"OK, OK, I do for you tomorrow," she said, bobbing her head like one of the laying hens, "but remember ..."

"I know. I have to believe," I said. "I do believe!" Baba dried her hands and rubbed her thumb across my cheek. I didn't have much feeling in the mole. My nerves were buried somewhere beneath the surface of it, but when Baba stroked, there seemed to be a prickly sensation. I didn't know if that was because her fingers were as rough as straw bales, or if there was some other reason. Like the fact that she hadn't once crocheted the wrong colour booties after she dangled a needle on a thread over the swell of a pregnant mother's belly. Baba claimed that kind of power came directly from God. I never dared ask how that could be. Once I asked her how Adam and Eve's children could marry each other and have babies if it was a sin for me to marry my own cousin. She got red in the face, sputtering strings of Ukrainian sentences: baler twine sentences that I couldn't comprehend. I did understand that the question had been a wicked one, and like a gnarled tangle, it tightened in my brain, unanswered.

After drying Baba's dishes, I went to bed early. I decided to pray. It was easy to pray in Baba's house. There were crucifixes in every room: copper, plastic, ceramic, and one made out of burnt and shellacked wooden matches. Da Vinci's *Last Supper* was reproduced three times in Baba's house. One had a mirror frame surrounding it. When I looked at it, I could see the lean of Christ's head and the mole on my cheek at the same time. At the bedside, I got down on my knees on the cold linoleum—just the way Baba did—placed the palms of my hands together, pointed to heaven and prayed for my own miracle.

The room was so dark Good Friday morning, it exerted a pressure, almost as firm as the touch of Baba's hand on my shoulder as she shook me awake.

"Come, ve go now. Must go before sun up."

I shivered out of my nightgown and into my pants and blouse, alert and listening for Mom's light snore in the next room. The old floorboards—silent under Baba's tread—creaked a path to the back door under me, even though I tensed every muscle to try and make myself lighter. Baba lit a kerosene lamp out on the step and the light spread through me like anticipation. A glowing circle defined us in the pre-dawn darkness as we started down the cattle path through the bush. The path was becoming narrower each year. Baba kept only one cow after Gedo died.

I harboured the secret idea that when we reached the creek, I would see something. A vision. I imagined that just like St. Bernadette's, the vision would be of the Virgin Mary and that perhaps right there on Baba's farm in Manitoba, a new Lourdes would emerge. The cattle path would be widened again from pilgrims and wheelchairs. There had been a few months when I had thought that living with the mole on my face would be fine. I would enter a convent and devote myself to Christ. Mom laughed out loud when I mentioned it one morning over a bowl of cereal.

"You have to be Catholic to be a nun!" Mom said.

"Aren't I Catholic?" I had asked, staring down at the mushy pile of golden flakes on my spoon.

"Greek Orthodox," Mom corrected.

"But we're not Greek," I said, frowning at the spoon.

"Go wash your face and get ready for school," Mom said.

As I struggled to keep up to Baba through the bare poplars, I remembered the week's horoscope from the *Chronicle*: "*Virgo:... The weekend brings major change.*" I knew that on Easter Sunday morning, when the mole was gone, I would have to make a decision: whether the miracle would be enough to convert me to Catholicism and a life of dedication to Christ, or whether I would get Suzie to hint around to Todd McCallister, who sat two rows over, to ask me to the spring prom. The prospect of having a choice was making my insides thresh against my ribs. I wondered how sinful it would be to choose both. I hoped that Baba couldn't hear the struggle in my soul as I followed her down the path.

At the creek she put down the lantern. "Is frozen," she said in a puff of visible breath. "Get me stick, Anna."

I found a large fallen branch and Baba poked it through the skim of ice at the bank's edge. The water gurgled up and floated over the sharp edges of ice. She cupped her hands, drew the water out and held the cold creek above my cheek. She let the water trickle out. I sucked air in between my teeth and squinted against the stinging iciness, but did not flinch away. She repeated this enough times for my cheek to start to throb with the cold. Then she crossed herself three times and I did the same. "*Vo Emnya Ocha. Eesino. Ee Schvatoho Doho. Ameen.*"

"Remember, Anna," she said, folding her arms over her chest, slipping her hands into the invisible space between her breasts and belly to rock out the numbness, "you have to believe."

I nodded and looked across the creek, checking for a sign. At that moment the eastern horizon split into light and darkness as the sun revealed itself over the lip of the field. My teeth started to chatter.

"Come Anna. Your jacket is vet."

By the time I was back under the paisley quilt in the corner bedroom, I was feverish. The next two days passed by in sips of ginger ale and dreams.

Mom is selling pysanka in the mall to pay for a plastic surgeon. She wants the same one that operates on Elizabeth Taylor. I come to the mall and show her that the mole has miraculously disappeared. Mom takes her egg money and chooses new Easter dresses and hats for both of us.

I opened my eyes to a dusky light to find Mom holding a cool washcloth on my forehead.

"Am I being punished?" I asked.

"No. You've got the flu!" Mom's bare face crinkled with concern and a thin smile. I could see the dark circles under her eyes which were usually covered with beige concealer. I smiled at her and drifted back to sleep, hoping to re-enter the dream.

I awoke clear-headed with the sun flooding through the window. Baba was standing in the doorway.

"Christ is risen," she said, her voice devoid of joy. Even before I reached up, I knew the exact spot where the single hair grew from it; I could feel, without moving my fingers, the familiarity of its pocked and ridged surface; I understood, without touching, that there was little feeling in it, that my nerves were still buried somewhere beneath its surface. I turned away from Baba to the blank of the wall. I could feel her eyes on me. I could sense they were wet like the drizzle in the *Old Country*.

Doing the Dance

"HOW WILL I KNOW IF IT'S THE *REAL* THING, MOM?" I WAS FOUR-teen years old and I was referring to love.

Mom gave me one of her looks, and I stopped chewing the inside corner of my mouth, sniffed, asked again, "No, really, Mom?"

She answered, "This cola is the real thing, Allie," and she splashed some into her tumbler of rum.

"I'm serious," I pleaded. She was still coherent and I hoped she might be talkative for a while.

She gulped down several swallows before replying, "I've never encountered the *real* thing. When I suspected it *wasn't* the *real* thing, I married your father anyway! Besides," she added, "what's *real* in this life? How do you know the grass under your feet is real, let alone airy-fairy *love*? Believe in your own reality, Allie. Matter of fact, believe in your own make-believe. Dance barefoot around the desert campfires in your head!" She stared into her tumbler, then added, "Your head's an oasis if you've got nowhere else to go. So dance there. Here's to your overactive imagination." She raised her drink to me in a toast and downed the remainder of the amber-black liquid.

I shambled, sulking, into my bedroom, back to whatever book I'd been reading, feeling as if Mom had let me down again. After she was no longer with me, about ten years later, I learned that her rum-laden advice could be as memorable as the final lines of a fable, as embraceable as an ancient proverb. It was lucky I got the phone call, or I might never have found that out.

"Allie Baird?" the voice on the telephone line said. "This is Olive at Flying Carpet Productions. We're offering you the role of the cocktail waitress in *The Summoned Nomad*. It's just the three lines you auditioned, but it's scale rates. We shoot Friday. Are you available?"

By the time I'd jotted down the particulars and hung up the phone, my feet were tapping out a victory dance. I didn't care if the smack of my high heels on my apartment's tired hardwood floor got the people who lived below me banging on their ceiling with a broom ... I had a speaking part in a feature film! Not enough to allow me to give up my day job doing make-overs at the cosmetic counter, but my first break!

My feet continued dancing as I dialled Vic's cell phone. I wanted him to be the first to know, couldn't wait to tell him. I was sorry I wouldn't see his tanned face break into a smile. I loved the way he looked at me: as if his eyes were measuring, calculating every corner of me—and then *shazzam*, his smile would break out like a completed renovation on his face. That's what happened the first day I met him: I was walking under his construction company's scaffolding on my way to work when a stray board broke free and just missed my head. Vic apologized and then, along with a dinner invitation, he offered me one of those smiles. I accepted. That was seven months earlier.

On the third ring, Vic answered his cell phone and I squealed into the receiver, "I got the cocktail waitress part!"

"No kidding?" he said. "Hey, that's great! When do you work?"

"Friday!"

"Friday?" He paused. I could hear pressurized banging in the background, pneumatic nailers. He added, "What about your computer course?"

My feet stopped. "Well ... Vic ... I'm not going to turn down my first real part because I have a computer class scheduled. I mean, I enrolled in it because you convinced me it was a good idea, and it is; but Rob Lampert is starring in this picture. I get to play my scene with *him*! I tell him to take a hike. How many actresses have done that? How many?"

"Allie, calm down! It's okay," Vic said. "But this computer course was what, just filling time for you?"

"Well, like you said Vic, *it was something to fall back on.*"

"Geez Allie, if I'd known you weren't interested, I wouldn't have paid for it." He sounded hurt.

I wrapped the telephone cord around my finger, watching the tip turn a bloated red. "It's not that I'm not interested, Vic, and like you said, *a computer course will never go to waste.* Besides I can pay you back now that I have this part."

"Don't be silly. I'm not going to take your money, Allie." His voice was all tense and wobbly; I'd never heard him sound that way.

Seven months wasn't that long, but I had a hard time remembering what my life felt like before Vic, as if that board had caused some kind of amnesia even though it missed my head. From that first dinner date, when I looked over at his strong, calloused hands wrapped around the stem of his wineglass, I had thought, could this be the real thing?

I heard Vic take a deep breath on the other end of the phone line, even though someone had started drilling in the background, and he said, "Well, I guess I'll see you Sunday?"

"Not until Sunday?" I asked.

"I'm leaving for the Builders' Convention in Vancouver, remember?"

"Oh, I forgot in all my excitement," I responded, disappointment cutting through me like a saw blade. "I was counting on you being around for moral support. I'm so nervous now."

"Hey," he said, sounding amused, the tension evaporated, "What's to be nervous about? It's not like a roof will cave in if you forget a line."

I laughed. It came out a limping twitter. "You're sweet, Vic," I said by way of apologizing for not giving his construction joke a big guffaw. I'd learned one thing about Vic, he took construction very seriously. If he was making a construction joke, it was for my benefit, to cheer me up. That was the great thing about Vic: he was ultra-focused on his career. Compared to him I was a dreamy dabbler—I couldn't even get my laugh to come out right. No wonder I was feeling nervous about my performance in *The Summoned Nomad*. I rocked from my toes onto the points of my high heels and back again, challenging myself to keep my balance and think of something clever to say to Vic.

"I know. I know," was all that came out, "I should stay positive, envision my goal, right?"

"Hang on a sec, Allie ... Hey Bart! That's the wrong casement ... Allie, listen, stop stressing yourself out. Turn down the role and join me in Vancouver for the weekend!"

I did laugh then. I guffawed.

"Hey, Allie-cat, I'm serious," he said in a low purr.

I loved it when he called me *Allie-cat*. I smiled into the receiver.

He continued, "A little of that balmy Vancouver sea air, a romantic restaurant overlooking the water, you never know what will pop into a guy's head under those circumstances."

I wasn't sure I'd heard the last sentence right over the buzz of a circular saw. "What did you say, Vic?"

"Do you want to come to Vancouver? Allie, are you still there?"

"Vic, I'd love to come. I mean I want to come. But all those auditions ... rejections ... I mean I've finally got a part." I imagined Vancouver harbour outside our hotel room window.

As Vic replied, the battery on his cell phone started to weaken. He was dropping out, "Hey, I'll bring y ... someth ... nice to wear fr ... ncouver. I'll ... e back ... day."

I couldn't tell if he sounded annoyed when half his words were missing. "What, Vic? I'm losing you, but I don't want to say goodbye," I whined, pressing the receiver to my ear, rubbing it nervously. "I just wish you could be with me on that movie set!"

There was loud static, followed by a *pfffttt!* sound and the line went dead.

I hung up the receiver and felt a hollow space under my ribs. Loneliness, dread, excitement poured into it like concrete into a form. To keep it from hardening, I spent the remainder of the week repeating my three scripted lines with every conceivable variation of expression. Out loud to my bedroom mirror, under my breath on the transit bus, in the bathroom with the words spitting out in a toothpaste foam, into the stacks of eyeshadow compacts on the shelves at work in a whispered hush, I repeated the words so often, they lost their meaning and sounded more like an incantation. I started to forget what the lines were, even though I'd easily memorized them. And all that time, I longed for Vic! As the cocktail waitress lines escaped me, his words replaced them...*you'll never know what will pop into a guy's head under those circumstances.*

Friday. Finally. I arrived on set and found it looked more like a construction site than a barroom. There were men and women hustling about with heavy tool belts hanging on their hips; electrical cords and equipment everywhere. A balding guy with a goatee, wearing a headset and carrying a clipboard, informed me he was Fezz, 3rd A.D.

"Fezz?" I verified.

"Yeah, short for Fred," he replied, "3rd Assistant Director." He whisked me off to the wardrobe trailer.

Two women, one with an opal stud in her lip, the other wearing about a hundred bracelets, handed me my minuscule cocktail waitress outfit.

Once I was dressed, the opal-studded one said, "Perfect!"

"Shows your great legs," agreed the braceleted one.

"The whole effect is so trampy."

"A little gold-digger-ish."

"So Jezebel."

Then they laughed so hard they had to hold onto each other to keep from falling down.

I tried my best to smile, but I was not getting the joke.

Fezz, 3rd A.D., knocked on the door and yelled over their laughter, "She can see Jade in make-up."

After every applied stroke of my make-up, Jade stopped and peered at her own bloodshot eyes in the mirror: "Gotta get sleep ... it's like sand scraping under my eyelids."

Fezz stuck his head into the hair and make-up trailer, jerked his thumb toward me and asked, "*She* ready?"

Jade blinked, squinted. "No! Give us a minute!"

A minute later, Fezz stuck his head in again. "*She* ready?"

I wanted to tell Jade I needed eyeliner, that I knew a little about make-up, but it seemed too presumptuous. I kept quiet while some woman, whose name I didn't catch, bobby-pinned a pouffe hairpiece to my head. It was obvious that the crew knew I was no top-billing, imported star. I did risk saying to Fezz, "Allie. My name's Allie."

"Right," he answered, checking his clipboard. Then he repeated, "*She* ready?" He didn't listen to the hair stylist's answer; instead, he pressed a switch on his walkie headset. "Copy that," he said into his microphone, then he pointed at me. "They're ready for you on set."

When I arrived back on set, a sultry-looking woman whispered to me, "Hi, I'm Ruby, 1st A.D. Eugene, our director, is over there with the star, Rob Lampert."

I looked over. Rob Lampert's back was to me. He looked shorter than I imagined and they'd lightened his hair for the role. He reminded me of Vic from behind, and I longed to be wrapped in Vic's arms, instead of standing there. Nothing in my numerous acting workshops had prepared me for the reality of being on set.

Eugene, the director—a gold hoop in one ear, a wisp of smoke curling around his head from his cigarette—came towards me. "Ah, our cocktail waitress!" his voice rumbled, "You will walk across the room with this drink tray, deliver your first two lines to

Rob Lampert, who of course is playing the title character and is intoxicated in this scene." He puffed a few times and continued, "After we complete the dolly shots and close-ups, we'll reset, moving to the door for your final line." Signalling the props man to put the drink tray on my hand, he asked, "Any questions?"

"Shouldn't I say hello to Rob Lampert before we start?"

Eugene, the director, was busy lighting another cigarette, but Ruby, 1st A.D., whispered, "No time. Behind schedule." Then she shouted, "Let's generate some atmosphere for the camera to take a look at. Quiet for rehearsal."

A machine belched artificial atmosphere smoke. My drink tray was heavy, my head felt weighed down by the pouffe, my throat was parched as if it had never tasted water, my wardrobe shoes pinched my toes; but I knew how to manage high heels at least from wearing them at work. It was the only familiar feeling I could hold onto as I walked across the room towards Rob Lampert's back.

I said my first line. "Last call."

"I'll have anotth-thher," came the slurred response of Rob Lampert.

Glasses slid off my tray and crashed to the floor.

"Vic!" I exclaimed as his familiar face—not Rob Lampert's—turned towards me. "What are you doing here?"

"Cut!" Eugene rumbled.

Two men swarmed around my feet, sweeping up the broken pieces as the props man replaced the glasses I'd broken. Vic turned his back to me.

Ruby, 1st A.D., shouted, "What's our cocktail waitress's second line?"

A mouse of a woman with a big black binder scurried towards me. "Your second line is, *I'll call you a taxi. You've had enough for one night.* O.K.?"

"But that's not Rob Lampert," I protested.

"Of course not," rumbled Eugene, the director, smoke circling his head. "He's the *Summoned Nomad*. Acting is transformation."

"No!" I insisted, "That's Vic. My boyfriend."

No one acknowledged my protest. Instead, they focused the camera on me, adjusted the lights on me, extended a tape measure from my face to the camera lens, and bobbed the microphone boom up and down over my head.

Ruby shouted, "Quiet for rehearsal. First positions."

"This is *unreal!*" I protested.

Everyone stared at me until I returned to my starting position.

"Atmosphere!" Ruby shouted.

Maybe it was the smoke machine that had affected me; maybe I hadn't seen right in the murky light.

"And action," Eugene rumbled.

I walked across the room. It was Vic. I said my line shaking my head, "Last call?"

Vic turned to me, slurring his words, "My god, Allie, look at you—as if acting wasn't enough prosss-tit-uting. Now you're working this sleazzze joint. Every guy in this dive is ogling you!" He waved his hand around, indicating the crew members. He continued, "I paid for that computer courssse. I told you I'd give you a decent, real job in my office when you were finisshhhed. But nooo-ooo."

"Vic, you're drunk!" I exclaimed.

He took a moment to measure my comment, then he smiled, one eyebrow arched.

"Wait," I said, steadying the drink tray on my shoulder, "is this some kind of reality TV show? No! I know! You went to all this expense to play a practical joke on me, right?"

Vic's smile turned into a scowl. "I've already thrown enough money after you to cover my company'sss payroll for a month," he answered.

"What?" I cried.

The mousy woman scurried over with her binder.

Eugene, the director, rumbled, "Just pick it up."

"Your line is—" the mousy woman squeaked.

"I know my line," I interrupted through gritted teeth. "Why isn't he saying the right lines?"

The mousy woman checked her binder. "His lines are correct."

"Cut!" Eugene strode towards me. He lowered his rumble, "It's natural to be nervous. Just let it go, relax." He made circles in the air with his hands, which dispersed more smoke from his cigarette.

"First positions," Ruby shouted. "We have to roll camera on this one . . . behind schedule. Final touches."

Jade from make-up stepped in, blinked her bloodshot eyes as she powdered my nose; while the woman whose name I didn't catch scrutinized the position of my hair pouffe.

"We're rolling," the cameraman stated.

"Sound?" Eugene rumbled.

"Speed."

"Slate?"

"Scene seventeen. Take one."

"And action," Eugene rumbled.

Walking across the room, I tried to reason it all out in my head. I could see the crew looking at me as if I was an idiot, an amateur. For some absurd reason, I felt my future career still rested on my performance.

"Last call," I said in a determined, cocktail-waitress voice.

"Ssssoo, are you going to let me take care of you?" Vic asked. "I know that'sss all you *really* want outta life. From the first time you accepted my dinner invitassshon I could tell you wanted macho and money. Opportunissst! That board was not going to hit you on the head. My men are careful. Ever sssso careful." He swallowed some of his drink, arched one eyebrow at me. "But watching you in your high heelsss on your way to work . . . jusssst looking at you was like rubbing my lamp!"

I delivered my line, "I'll call you a taxi. You've had enough for one night."

"Cut," rumbled Eugene. "Very nice! Check the gate."

We replayed the scene again and again, from different camera angles; each time Vic varied his lines. Once he delivered the cliché that I'd never make it without him. In between shots while the crew repositioned, I tried to speak to Vic privately, but Fezz, 3rd A.D., whisked him off set, and I was stranded with the craft services people who lavished cut-up fruit and mini-falafels on me. I didn't feel compensated.

"Where do they take him?" I muttered out loud as I sucked on a grape.

A tall woman with a long thin braid, who was toting bottled water, answered me, "Back to his Winnebago."

She seemed receptive to my question, so I asked her another, "Why is he saying all those things that aren't in the script?"

"I don't know what this movie is about," she said. "I just do the liquid beverages, hot and cold, and the cookies and gum and small snacks." She smiled.

Thwarted, I waited for my final close-up. When the camera was rolling, Vic actually uttered another line from the script, "You can call me a taxi assss long assss you're coming home with me, baby."

Satisfaction coursed down to my toes as I delivered my final line, "Get real. Take a hike, buddy!"

Eugene rumbled, "And cut!" He ground out his cigarette. "Excellent! Check the gate."

The crew erupted into spontaneous applause.

"Gate's clean," someone responded.

"That's a picture wrap for Allie Baird," Ruby shouted.

More applause; then Fezz, 3rd. A.D., whisked me off set to the hair and make-up trailer.

As the nameless hairstylist was removing my pouffe, the door swung open and in sauntered Rob Lampert who dropped into the chair next to mine. He was tall and had dark hair.

"Great work today, Allie," he said.

"Yes...uh...you too."

He smiled, one eyebrow arched. "Nice chemistry. You brought a lot of emotion to our work—made it real."

"Uh...thanks," I said. I leaned as close as I dared to sniff for liquor on his breath. There was a hint of spicy aftershave emanating from him.

"I hope our paths cross again," he said, kissing my cheek. He swung out the trailer door, letting in a gentle breeze.

I left shortly afterwards. Alone. The evening slant of sunlight was vivid after the murkiness on set. I slid my feet out of my high heels and stepped onto the boulevard. The concrete curb held the day's warmth, the grass was cool and soothing. I walked a short distance then raised my arms above my head, pointed a toe, kicked up one leg, half-expecting to conjure a mirage. Instead, there were sparrows chirping as an orange transit bus lumbered past. I continued walking. Mom's advice came back to me, and I understood the benefit of doing the dance in my head—at times, it can be the only guide to what's real.

Meltdown

I WAS IMMERSED IN A THICK ROMANCE NOVEL ABOUT A DANCEHALL girl who finds true love during the Klondike gold rush, when Cal Carmack phoned asking if we had room in our freezer for some extra ice cream. Without thinking, I said, "Sure!" There was always room in our freezer: Ronald insisted on having the maximum cubic-foot model so we could buy bulk and save. As I hung up the phone, I realized I should have been paying more attention and asked Cal Carmack why he was involving us in his ice cream surplus. We barely knew Cal and Julie. They were just neighbours down the street—acquaintances. The door bell rang before I could phone him back. I opened the front door and the afternoon sun blazed in. I blinked, squinted. I'd had the curtains closed all afternoon because last year Ronald insisted if he was going to pay for new carpets, I'd better protect them against fading. The early June day had grown unseasonably hot, while I'd been lost to a Yukon blizzard.

Cal Carmack stood on my front step holding two large plastic pails in each hand. He wore a baseball cap, turned backwards, which held his curly, caramel-coloured hair in check. He smiled, nodded as if he meant to remove his hat but his hands were full. I noticed his even white teeth. Perfect teeth, I thought to myself, then remembered that his wife, Julie, was a dental hygienist.

"That's a lot of ice cream," I observed.

His smile faded. He looked down at the pails, pumped them up and down as if he was guessing their weight, then said, "Actually there's more in the truck, if you've got the space."

I wished I hadn't made him feel awkward. I tried to restore his ease, "Sure, it's not like storing an igloo or something!"

His smile returned. His head tilted back as if he was about to roar with laughter, but there was just a smile. I reached for the pails. We fumbled with the metal handles. Carrying them to the freezer, I felt the frosty chill through my jeans. At the front door, Cal held four more pails. I could hear a soft dinging sound caused by the keys in his truck ignition; his radio twanged out a country and western tune.

He said, "I should carry these down for you. They're heavy."

"Hey, I'm a strong farm girl!"

"I didn't mean . . . ," he started, paused, restarted, ". . . Julie complains that because I move people's furniture for a living, I expect her to lug heavy stuff, too."

I nodded, feeling the metal handles dig into my fingers. While he was in the explaining mood, I should have asked him where the ice cream came from and why he was bringing it to us. Before I could, he turned his baseball cap around, tipped it slightly in a kind of salute and said, "Well, thanks, Victoria. Hope you and your boys enjoy it!" Then he strode to his truck as if he was afraid I'd change my mind.

I put the pails down and smoothed my hair as I watched him back out of the driveway. He didn't notice me wave.

One half of my freezer was now full to the top, but I closed the lid and hurried back to my book before my boys tumbled in the front door from school. It wasn't until later, when Ronald came home from work, and, tie loosened, headed straight for the freezer to get ice for his gin and tonic, that I thought about the ice cream again. Ronald's voice carried up the stairs. "What the heck's this?"

The boys, who were setting the table, snapped to attention, glancing at each other to see which one of them was in trouble.

Winded from the flight of stairs, Ronald asked between huffing breaths, "Victoria, why'd you buy all that ice cream?"

The boys looked relieved, happy even.

As I explained, Ronald slammed the bag of ice into the sink to break it apart, then he said, "Carmack? What's he doing? Hosting his daughters' baseball wind-up?" He poured more than a jigger's worth of gin over the ice.

"Hey, I think I'll have one of those too," I said, hoping to sidetrack him. "Celebrate the summer-like weather."

"Mom, when can we have some ice cream?" the boys chorused.

Ronald answered, "It's not ours."

I said, "Well, actually it must be. Cal said he hoped the boys would enjoy it."

I reached for the drink Ronald had mixed, but he didn't relinquish it. "Did you pay him for it?" he demanded.

"No."

"What are we? A charity case?" he roared. "We hardly know the guy! Why the heck would he give us thirty-two litres of the stuff?"

I stepped forward, took my drink. Ronald had actually calculated the number of litres we'd acquired! I sucked an ice cube from my drink and crunched it between my teeth. "I don't know, Ronald." I sighed, baffled.

"It's probably stolen!" Ronald declared.

"Oh, Ronald." I countered with a suggestion, "Big moving companies like the one Cal works for refuse to move freezer contents. Maybe one of his customers offered it to him. He brought it home and Julie refused to keep it because it's not the best way for teeth to get their calcium!" I raised my gin and tonic to Ronald for a toast.

He ignored my gesture. "Well, we don't know where that ice

cream's been, and since I'm on the road for a week starting tomorrow, you'll have to get rid of it yourself, Victoria!"

The boys knew not to protest. I took my cue from them. "Okay, I'll get rid of it," I agreed.

After Ronald fell asleep that night, I slipped out from between the sheets, snuck a spoon, and crept down the basement stairs, sticking to the sides of the treads so that they wouldn't squeak. I thought back to a time when Ronald didn't complain that ice cream gave him gas, when we stopped for double scoops at Ice Maid, or strolled through Little Italy with a bowl of gelati. Ages ago. Another lifetime.

The freezer door opened with a visible puff of frosty air. I lifted the top flavour—Raspberry Ripple—and peeled back the lid. It crackled. Standing still, I listened for Ronald's footsteps overhead. The only sound was the hum of the freezer motor. I lowered my nose and sniffed. It smelled good—fresh and rasp-berryish. I inspected the other flavours: Chocolate, Bubble Gum, Vanilla, Butterscotch, Strawberry, Black Licorice, Rocky Road.

I sampled the Strawberry first, thinking about what kind of man brings volumes of ice cream to a neighbour he hardly knows. The spoon bent as I dug into the cold, creamy surface. My tongue, teeth, and forehead ached from the chilly delicious-ness of the first mouthful. I wondered if Cal Carmack had been the lanky teenager who pedalled the Icy Nice cart around my cousins' neighbourhood the summer I was ten and came to the city to visit. The tinkling bell was the most wondrous sound I'd ever heard. It meant that ice cream on sticks could be delivered to where you waited on the sidewalk. No milking the cows, no turn-ing the crank on the ice-cream maker. Maybe Cal never got over that look of delight on kids' faces as they lined up for their turn, quarters clutched in their sweaty fingers. Perhaps, as an adult, Cal actually bought ice cream and randomly delivered it for the pure pleasure. Maybe in mid-life, giving away frozen dairy prod-ucts had become a spiritual experience for him, more satisfying than sex with his dental hygienist wife.

A hunger deepened in me. I craved the knowledge of Cal

Carmack's ice cream. With Ronald gone for the week, I reasoned, maybe I could find a way to uncover the mystery of it. I opened the Black Licorice and skimmed my spoon across its tenebrous centre swirl. Sitting on the cold, concrete basement floor, in front of my white freezer, staring at the red indicator light that warned against power outages and a potential thaw, I exchanged one flavour for the next until I had sampled them all. When I finally crawled back into bed beside my husband, my lips were sweetened with pasture and sugar, my breath soured with guilt.

The next morning, with the kids off to school, I walked up the street, and down the back lane. Cal was spraying fertilizer on his lawn. Later, when I spied his truck driving down the street, I hopped in my car, followed him to the dry cleaners and hardware store. He was on days off. I forced myself not to trail him right up his driveway. After school, I fed the kids triple scoops of Bubble Gum and made them swear they wouldn't tell their father when he returned home.

The following morning, the radio predicted another scorching high of 29 degrees Celsius. Cal was out early trimming his hedge. By 10:00 a.m., I was following him across the city. He stopped at an older sub-division strip mall and entered a small shop with a loopy neon sign, *Carmie's Cones*. Sitting in my car, air-conditioner running, I watched an older couple greet him with hugs and cups of coffee. They sat on delicate wrought iron chairs and chatted. No other customers. I could imagine the line-ups later: hot weather, brisk business.

That evening, the boys invited their soccer teams for Chocolate cones. I calculated that even at that rate, we couldn't consume all the evidence before Ronald returned. I should have been satisfied now that I knew where it came from. I wasn't. One part of me wanted to settle for purging the freezer, returning to normal. Another part of me craved more, relished the heightened awareness in me, basked in my own feverish heat. Later in bed, I dreamt that Ronald and I were camping near the Arctic. It was midnight, still light. I crawled into our tent to sleep. Cal Carmack was there. I was happy to see him. I wondered, without it really mattering, why Ronald was gone. Cal opened a container of what appeared to be snow, but I knew it wasn't. We bent our heads over it; on our hands and knees we lapped at it as if we were sled dogs, our tongues touching now and again. A warm pleasure pulsed through me as I woke up. I crept down to the freezer and cooled off with mouthfuls of Butterscotch. The flavour tasted overly bright—a sun that wouldn't set.

When Cal's truck left his driveway around noon the next day, I followed him across the city again. At first I thought we were headed for Carmie's Cones, but we took a different route and pulled into the Rodeo Bar and Grill. It sported a hitching post out front and a windowless façade. It made no sense to wait outside. Dark roughened wood and leather saddles decorated the walls. When my eyes adjusted to the dimness I saw Cal sitting at the saloon-style bar. A song about someone's *deceivin' heart* crooned on the sound system and accompanied me across the floor. For a moment I was close enough to touch the back of Cal's neck with my fingertips. I hoisted myself onto the stool next to him and said a quiet, "Hey, there."

His initial look of shock dissolved into inscrutability. My name was on his lips but he shut them before the word came out. He nodded slowly. The bartender put a glass of draught in front of him and I said I'd have the same.

After the bartender served my beer and moseyed away, Cal asked, "What are you doing here?"

"I haven't been quite myself since the ice cream arrived," I offered as an explanation.

When he didn't respond, I found myself looking at the rows of shining bottles behind the bar, at the lights on the video lottery terminals as they spun their fruits and sevens past the lunch patrons.

He tried again. "Why are you *really* here?" His fingertips tapped in nervous repetition on the side of his glass.

"I just wanted to know why you gave it to us."

He swivelled on his stool, glanced towards the door, then said, "You followed me here to ask me that?"

I nodded.

He drank his beer, wiped a bit of foam off his upper lip. I had the urge to reach over and do that for him, but he started his explanation.

"My folks own an ice-cream shop. Mom, who's been worrying about memory loss lately, made a mistake, double-ordered in the wrong containers. She didn't want Dad to know. I took the extra so he wouldn't find out." He paused, then slipped his hand over the back of my stool, and said intimately, "I'm sorry if this somehow got you involved, Victoria." He added, "We were out of space in our freezer. You were the only neighbour home at the time."

My eyes drifted to his furniture-moving, muscled forearm. I took frenzied gulps of beer and thought, *A mere convenience, nothing more.*

Out loud, I said, "You don't think it'd be prudent for your mother to tell him, rather than keep it hidden?"

He looked into his empty glass. "Marriages have secrets. Are you going to tell your husband what you did this afternoon?"

Heat surged to my cheeks. I reached for a ten-dollar bill in my purse. "Hey, let me buy your beer to say thanks for the ice cream." I put the bill on the counter. I wasn't sure of his intention, nor of mine.

After a moment, he picked up the ten and curled it back into my hand. "Victoria," he started, "until you peel back the lid and take a taste, you can't be sure you'll enjoy a new flavour. Even though it's ice cream, it can be disappointing. Stick with Vanilla. That's my philosophy."

I nodded, felt dismissed. I smiled a weak goodbye. "Thanks for the ice-cream advice," I said before I walked to the door. The parking lot was sweltering; the interior of my car, smelter-hot. I switched the air-conditioner to high and drove aimlessly around the block numerous times, not knowing what to do, where to go next. That's when I noticed Cal's truck turning ahead of me into the Roadside Inn. I caught a glimpse of a blonde woman in the cab. It wasn't Julie. The Raspberry Ripple I'd eaten for breakfast began to curdle from the beer I'd just downed. I leaned my head back and thought about how ice cream transcends an ordinary day. It's a shame how quickly you get your fill.

Jackpot Jungle

YOU KNOW, EVER SINCE ALBERT DIED, I'VE BEEN FEELING THAT his soul is inhabiting a VLT at the McPhillip's casino—a Jackpot Jungle slot—the kind that takes up to three quarters. Did you know you should always play the maximum number of quarters? Then, if you hit the jackpot, you get a bigger payout!

The thing is, I always wanted to go to Africa. Now, don't get me wrong, I'm not knocking Albert. He took me places: up to Gimli for the drag races, into the Whiteshell to camp. But I was always so busy filling coolers and emptying coolers and worrying whether the potato salad had gone bad and chasing flies off the tops of Albert's bottles. Oh, that used to really bug me! Albert never cared whether the flies were sipping his beer. Then, after he'd have a few, he'd get to feeling romantic and start kissing me with lips that had licked fly footprints off beer bottles. Flies like to land on dog shit. You know what I mean? There must be flies in Africa. They've got those tsetses that carry sleeping sickness, don't they? I don't like to think about that. I just imagine the sun coming up all pink and golden, and the giraffes' long necks silhouetted against the sky next to those spreading trees that look like broccoli spears. Wouldn't it be great to go explore there, wearing one of those khaki-coloured outfits and a smart-looking safari hat covering up your perm gone-to-frizz, with binoculars and one of those huge cameras that *National Geographic* photographers sling around their necks? Just pile into a jeep and head straight into that heat wave shimmer!

I shouldn't complain. Albert didn't share my interest in Africa, but he never beat me. He never raised his voice much even. He wasn't mean to our kids; cheap maybe, but never mean. So I can't explain why my shoulders tensed up to my ears when he came home from the rail yards and flopped in front of the TV each day. I'd burn supper. I'd yell at Savannah and Leo. Some nights I never stopped yelling until they'd said their prayers and were fast asleep, and then I'd look in on them, sniff the clean cotton pyjamas smell of them and I'd feel my throat tighten so I'd have just enough breath to ask myself, "Maxine, Maxine, what the hell is the matter with you?"

That's what convinced me that Albert's soul is in that Jackpot Jungle. Every time I go near that terminal, my shoulders tense up to my ears. I think his spirit is feeling guilty about something, wanting to make amends.

Don't tell my kids. Savannah's stressed with her twins, and Leo with his first promotion . . . I don't want them worrying that their mother is a crackpot. But something tells me that Jackpot Jungle is going to start paying me big and you know what? I'll be on the first plane to Africa.

Mining It (For All It's Worth)

KELLY DOESN'T TELL HANK'S STORY UNLESS SOMEONE BUYS A round for her table. Like a guarded geologist, she is only willing to reveal her core samples to potential investors. The locals don't offer anymore, but summer brings wilderness-adventure tourists curious about the area's lore, and seasonal fire-fighter recruits with high wages burning holes in their pockets.

Once the tall glasses of draught arrive, Kelly begins, "I was at work, reducing the price on steel-toed boots, when old Stu, the cherry flashing red on top of his cruiser, strode in, said, 'Kelly, you better come with me to the mine pit.'"

She pauses here, drags on her cigarette, swallows some beer. That's the pace she maintains: a few sentences—small pellets of detail—a swig and a drag, as if there's no rush to tell it. (As if by taking her time, she can delay last call at the Hematite Hotel; delay the solitary trek home and the onset of longings as steep as the sides of the hole that Hank dug.)

"Protesting," Kelly explains to the out-of-towners. "Hank wasn't just pissin' around when he dug that hole." She tells them her husband was taking a stand against the closing of the Hematite Mine, the folding up of people's lives in a place where the steady diet was iron ore—raw ore, chewed out of the side of the landscape, cooked, shaped, and shipped east to satisfy some steelworks' hunger. "And yeah, maybe our stacks belched arsenic or asbestos or something, but people here had to feed their kids too, you know?"

She squints around the table and dares the canoe-trip naturalists and fire-fighter ecology majors to defy her. They don't. She's still a looker, but it's more than that. It's as if the sign on the outskirts of town reads:

Welcome to the Hematite Iron Range
Don't Rile the Locals

"No one," continues Kelly, "remembers Hank for his heroism. All graveyard shift, he dug with that loader. In the morning he claimed he wouldn't budge from his hole until the CBC did a story about the town's plight. That's when that airhead Adriana, the union's secretary, started running around the top edge of the hole. She was weeping, begging him to come up, calling him *Hankie*. If it wasn't for her, they'd have canonized Hank: Saint Hank of Hematite." Kelly pauses before she adds, "Imagine a town this size, and no one knew Hank and Adriana were screwing around behind my back until that day."

Kelly's nostrils flare as she blows cigarette smoke. She tips back the last of her beer, then continues, "The banks of that hole weren't stable. I arrived just as the slide started and saw Adriana topple in, high heels and all. They estimated ninety ton on top of the two of them. After the funerals, the entire town dumped Hank's martyrdom on me—his wronged widow."

Kelly holds her lips around the word *widow*; makes it sound like an empty glass; excavates another round.

Shorn

MY COUSIN MANDY WAS A BEAUTY QUEEN. WHEN WE WERE SMALL, I was acutely aware of the differences between us. We were the same height, born in the same month of the same year, but Mandy's hair cascaded over her shoulders in a long blonde sweep that seldom tangled from its smooth lustre, even when we climbed trees. Mother kept my own dark, thick hair cropped short because I detested the brushing and because she said it wouldn't hang in the way while I did chores. "Chickens will peck at dangling hair; they'll think it's a worm," she'd warn. She sometimes mentioned head lice if I requested to grow it out. Mandy's face also demanded your attention. I suppose that was due to its near-perfect symmetry, but at the time, all I knew was that I longed to just gaze at her. My own face was asymmetrical. Cut down the middle, my face could have been perceived as belonging to two different people: one cheekbone a little higher than the other, one half of my bottom lip a fraction thicker than the other side. When I asked my mother how she and her sister could look so much alike, while Mandy and I were born so different, she replied, "I suppose it's because your Aunt Eileen married a Swede."

"That's like Dad having his prize bull, then?"

Mother laughed. "Cammie, you are as bright as your cousin is pretty," she said.

That seemed enough of a link in those early years because despite our physical differences, Mandy and I were inseparable. Although Mandy's family lived in the city, Uncle Olas, an airline captain, was seldom home, so Aunt Eileen and Mandy were frequent weekend guests at our farm. Mandy loved the tree swing my father built, and she always asked me to pick her berries from my mother's garden. She taught me how to braid her hair and make clothes for the paper dolls she brought along, packed into her very own matching luggage. I was good at colouring the new outfits and cutting them out precisely. Mandy designed them and marked them with tiny pencil letters, indicating which colours I was to use in which places: *B* for blue on a sleeve, *PP* for purple on the bodice. It was my responsibility to carefully erase the letters before I coloured. When it was time for me to do my chores, Mandy would abandon her sandals and dress shoes to wear one of the many pairs of rubber boots in our closet. She trailed along with me, revealing the secrets of her city girlfriends, like Ruthie, whose father took off to the Yukon with the kindergarten teacher, and Kate, whose mother kept a bottle of vodka in the bedside table. While Mandy gossiped, I fed and watered the animals or gathered eggs (sure to miss one or two on those days), and gave only a passing pat to the calves and lambs which would otherwise have received all of my attention. Mandy never helped and ignored the animals completely.

When I finished my chores Mandy always said, "I really have to go to the bathroom."

"The outhouse is closest," I would say.

"I hate the outhouse. Come with me," she'd insist.

I'd put down my buckets and trudge behind her. At the outhouse door, she'd wrinkle her nose and brandish her hand at the flies.

"Camille," she'd beg, "please hold my hand, so I don't fall in." I'd hold her hand until the hollow echo of her stream ended and she hopped off the threatening hole. I never thought to betray her trust—a quick jerk of my hand to tip her backwards, off-balance, hear her city scream. It never entered my mind.

Mandy won her first city-wide pageant at age eleven. *The Little Miss Pretty and Talented Contest.* They came to our farm the weekend following her victory, even Uncle Olas joined them. I overheard Aunt Eileen confide to my mother that Mandy had beat twelve-year-olds who were already *fully developed* to capture the title. Uncle Olas had newspaper clippings—a copy for everyone—of Mandy's crowned head and royal smile. He had handwritten the date on all the articles so we would never lose track. *Mandy Andersson,* the article stated, *tap-danced her way through the talent portion and right into the hearts of the judges.* To compensate for his absence in Hawaii during the actual judging, and to encourage her dancing talent, Uncle Olas had brought Mandy back a genuine grass skirt and island print bikini top from Hawaii. My brothers and I received plastic leis. Thankful to be included in the exotic nature of his travels and Mandy's successes, we tried the hula dance. Even my two brothers joined in; but no one except Mandy could make her hips move the right way. I thought it was just because she was in possession of the skirt which none of the adults insisted she share. Mother acknowledged it was her dance training. Aunt Eileen beamed. Uncle Olas sucked in his thin cheeks at the sight of her. Father went out to milk. And my brothers shifted towards a necessary avoidance of our cousin. Mandy's grass skirt had ignited in them like a stubble fire on a windy night. Their herds grazed on her grass skirt. Her grass skirt became the source of smudge smoke in their hours surrounding dusk.

Later on that hula night, squished beside me in my narrow single bed, Mandy whispered, "Some of it depends on how you look at the judges. You have to imagine the right thing in your head so that the expression on your face is something they'll respond to. If they're women judges you imagine that you've dusted their coffee tables. If there are some men, then you have to adjust. You imagine you've stolen their wallets and bought yourself new underwear with their money."

"Mandy, oooohh," I squealed so that there were *shut ups* hissed from my brothers' room.

"Oh Camille," she said as if I was so very naive, "it's just a trick I discovered. Trick of the trade. Obviously it works. I'm the winner." Then just as Mandy was drifting off into her easy and deep sleep, she yawned through her words, "Camille, your hair always smells like the barn. Mother says it's because farm people don't bathe as much as we do."

Her breathing shifted and Mandy was asleep, her hair spread out around her as if brushed into place on the white pillow. There was a bold moonlight that night and it illuminated her blonde hair into a ghostliness, a holiness. A small piece of wayward grass from the skirt nested near her scalp. I picked it out. She didn't stir. I lifted a long strand of her hair and fingered its fineness. I pressed it to my nose and breathed in the scent of early morning clover and dewy grass. Mandy's hair did not smell of the barn, even though she had been there that afternoon. I couldn't manage to get a whiff of my own hair. It slipped out of my fingers as I tugged it towards my nostrils. I had to take Mandy's word for it. I crept downstairs and washed my hair in the kitchen sink; rinsed out the shame; wrapped my plastic lei around my fingers in endless cat's cradle and waited for my hair to dry.

After that we didn't see Mandy on the weekends any more. She was busy in her poise and modelling classes. She came at Easter and Christmas and for a few days of summer vacation and we wrote to each other. In her letters, I didn't notice how her posture had altered; how her walk had transformed into a sway that made her hair swing gently from side to side. And it was easy in letters to ignore Mandy's new way of talking with you: she looked slightly to one side of you as if there were cue cards just behind one of your ears which she could read if she lost her place in the conversation. This gave her the advantage of being able to see if someone more interesting entered the room. She could

smile convincingly when she didn't mean it, and this also could
not be detected on paper. It was easier to be with Mandy in her
letters.

I didn't have much time to miss her. My two older brothers
went away to university. With the boys gone, my mother's work
load lessened while my father's increased, so I was encouraged to
do more outdoor chores. The next years passed in the day-to-day
of milking and separating; and in the seasonal shifts of shearing
the winter off the sheep, hand-feeding the new calves and lambs
which had no one to suckle them; learning to drive the combine
for the last of the harvest.

The spring that Mandy and I turned fifteen, the women's aux-
iliary, of which my mother was the president, schemed up a fund-
raiser that would help send our 4-H club to the Brandon Winter
Fair the following year.

"Mother," I said when she returned from her meeting, "*4-H
Queen* is the stupidest thing I ever heard of. I'm not having any-
thing to do with it."

"You have to participate, Cammie, or you won't be allowed to
go with the group. The boys split firewood this past winter,
remember? Now it's the girls' turn. You will be divided into
teams. Team leaders, one of which will be you, Cammie, will be
princesses. For two months all the girls will sell buttons for their
princess leader. The community members buy a button for the
princess of their choice. The team that sells the most buttons,
wins. That princess will be crowned Queen at a social and dance.
Simple."

I expected my father to support my protest, but when he came
into the house wiping the grease off his hands from a tractor
repair, he said, "We'll show your Aunt Eileen she's not the only
one with a beauty queen daughter, eh?"

Although I had observed that Mandy and I were unlike each
other, I had never before felt the need for me to be different.
Until that moment. A quack-grass system of jealousy spread
through me; long, anemic-looking, tough, fibrous roots of envy.
My refusal to sell buttons became steadfast. It was my way of

refusing to compete with Mandy on her turf. A way of saying I didn't value the popular and pretty race that button sales would reflect. The buttons read *4-H Princess Who will be Queen?* Stickers with the princesses' names were attached accordingly. Mother insisted my sticker read *Camille*, even though all the people around called me *Cammie*.

Girls on my team would report in giggles, "We were selling outside the Co-op, and Mr. Lind came out with a bag of seed, looked at the buttons and said, 'Who the hell's Camille?' We told him. 'Oh *Cammie!*' he said, putting the seed down and digging into his pocket. He bought two buttons 'cause he was so embarrassed, he didn't know—living on the next farm from you all this time—that you had a real name. That's what he said—*a real name!*"

Mother was furious at my refusal to sell buttons. Every time she went to town, she came back with information on the tally and the fact that I wasn't doing my part and that it was rumoured that Tracy Tate was at least fifty buttons ahead. The more she badgered me, the less I came out of the barn. She'd call me but I'd pretend I couldn't hear her over the scraping sounds. We had the cleanest stalls that spring. I began to appreciate the weight of straw and sheep and cow dung on the end of a shovel. I noticed after a few weeks it felt lighter even though the shovelfuls were fuller. I was beginning to develop shoulders like the swimmers you see in the Olympic heats. That was when Neil Lind started to come by. Pinned to his jacket was one of the buttons his father had bought outside the Co-op: *Camille*. He'd pick up a shovel when I ignored him and he'd help me clean the stalls. If he stopped to rest on his shovel or pitchfork, there was an observant stillness to him that made me work faster.

After the barn was clean, sometimes we'd play with the twin lambs whose mother had died giving birth to them and who had to be bottle fed, or we'd sit on one of the fence rails of the corral, watch our old sway-back mare swish her tail and we'd talk about school and 4-H, while the meadowlarks announced *I-was-here-a-year-ago* in the cool spring evening. Neil agreed with me that the whole business of a 4-H Queen was pretty lame, but it would help out financially. He said he'd take some buttons to sell to the guys on his fastball team, though not to Larry because he was selling them for Wanda, even though Wanda probably didn't stand a chance. Sometimes during our talks, Neil sat so close I caught the scent of Irish Spring soap mixed with the signature of his sweat, and I had to hold the fence post tighter to keep from slipping off.

Mother stopped calling me in, went to town every Saturday morning to sell buttons, sewed me a dress that looked like an extravaganza, and one evening announced that Aunt Eileen, Uncle Olas and Mandy would be attending the social and crowning. I didn't take notice of what she said because that was the same evening that Neil had asked, "I was wondering if you needed a ride to the social?" He said it without looking at me, his eyes fixed at a point in the pasture behind the barn where the spring lambs followed their mothers and bleated.

I didn't know how much I wanted to ride with him until, just as the sun dipped below the tree line, he kissed me. First with his lips, but a moment later with his whole body, his arms pulling me up against him until a richness, as sweet as Mother's caramel custard, spread through me.

On the night of the social and queen crowning, Mandy, Aunt Eileen and Uncle Olas arrived just in time for dinner. Aunt Eileen brimmed with excitement. She had brought a bag full of discarded costume jewellery for me to paw through in case there was something that matched my dress. Mandy pointed out why she didn't need the trinkets any more: she had received so much real jewellery as prizes at her beauty competitions. Mother rushed around getting dinner laid out for everyone.

There was enough chatter around the dining room table that no one noticed I couldn't eat my meal. Each mouthful lodged in my throat so that I pushed my plate away after a few attempts. It hadn't been until Mandy was in the same room with me that I realized that not to win the crown would be humiliating. And I began to wonder if Neil would be embarrassed when I lost as well. Ever since he had kissed me there was a part of him left behind, an imprint on my being that I could wear, flaunt even, as visible as his wiry body, as particular as his scent, more decorative than any bag of costume jewellery. In return, I felt as if I had to take Neil's opinions and feelings into account; because now that I had something that I hadn't known I needed before, I wanted to keep it.

Aunt Eileen cut into my thoughts, "Olas had the Lincoln waxed so that we could drive Cammie to her crowning in style! I'm afraid it's gotten dusty on the way. The roads are dreadful! You need some rain."

Mother straightened her shoulders. "Actually, Cammie has an escort for the evening." She gave a quick sniff at the end of the statement.

"Aaah-ha!" Uncle Olas said with a wink at my brothers who were also home from university.

"A date?" Aunt Eileen's eyebrows almost sprang up to her hairline. "But Mandy's come all this way…" Her voice trailed off and she looked at my father.

"If I could trouble you to pass the gravy, Eileen," he said.

Mandy sat demurely as if the emotions raging around the table didn't trouble her, then she said, "I can ride with Camille and her boy, Mother." Her eyes settled on me the way a butterfly lands on a flower then skips ahead. "I'm sure Camille won't mind."

"Excellent idea," Aunt Eileen nodded. "Mandy can chaperone," she pointed out to my mother.

My dress spread across the front seat of Neil's pickup, obscuring the stick shift and getting caught on Mandy's high heels. Mandy's dress took up no extra space in the cab. Neil's fingers drummed on the steering wheel and he bobbed back and forth to look past me out the passenger side window as if he were checking crops. Most weren't planted yet, nothing to see but the deep, dark furrows in the loam. The truck interior smelled like last year's hay and Mandy's perfume. My brain screamed for conversation, but everything Neil and I would have said to each other seemed wrong with Mandy in the truck.

Mandy said, "So have you prepared something to say when you win?"

"I doubt if I'm going to win," I replied, running my hands over the lap of my dress to try and keep it from puffing up.

"Winning wasn't really the point to this contest," Neil joined in.

I wanted to slip my arms through his at that moment.

"Winning is always the point!" Mandy said and laughed. "That's why it's a contest!"

The truck hit washboard on the gravel road and the vibrations shook us into an unfillable chasm of silence until we reached the social. Inside, the hall was festooned with streamers and garlands and our 4-H banner. Two fiddlers were on stage tuning up their instruments, and the foggy haze from cigarettes was settling in. My brothers joined us at a table and Neil plied them with questions about campus life. Then Neil insisted we dance the butterfly and even Mandy came back to the table breathless and flushed.

At eleven o'clock, with the five princesses lined up on stage, and me with my heart unexpectedly pounding in my ears, they made the announcement, naming the runners-up in ascending order. I expected to hear my name each time, but the last. "...and that means that Camille Landry is Queen of the 4-H club!" There were hoots and whistles and loud applause. Someone placed a tiara on my head, a bouquet of flowers in my arms. I said thank-you, but couldn't feel my legs. Somehow I got off the stage and a swarm of people, including my mother and father, came to hug me, congratulate me, say how beautiful I was in my dress. By the time I returned to our table, even my brothers were grinning at me. I hadn't known that winning something that you despised could feel so good. Then I noticed the two empty chairs.

"Where are Neil and Mandy?" I asked, trying to keep my smile in place.

My brothers shrugged. One of them said, "They were here while you were up on stage."

They returned at midnight.

Neil strutted up to me and said, "Hey, way to go there, Cam!"

"Where were you?" I asked as if I was certain of my right to ask it.

"Already acting like a queen!" Mandy said and looked to my brothers for approval.

Neil replied, "Mandy was feeling queasy with all the smoke in here." I stared at him and he looked down at his boots for a moment. When he looked back up he was gazing at Mandy. "Out for a breath of fresh air," he added.

When I turned away from him and headed to the buffet table, he followed me into the cold-cut line. Mandy remained with my brothers. She was lecturing them about how eating late at night was the worst for weight gain.

Neil said to me, "I guess you're pretty pleased with yourself."

I held my head up. I didn't want him to see how his absence had affected me. When I replied, I tried to make myself sound like Mandy, "It feels better than I thought it would."

One of the ladies' auxiliary workers, who was refilling the dill pickles, interrupted with a toothy smile: "I bought your button. I thought you'd win, Cammie!"

Neil leaned his head towards me and muttered at my ear, "Yeah, well none of the other girls have a rich uncle!"

I wheeled around, "What?"

Neil smirked. "Mandy told me. You don't have to pretend."

"Pretend what?" I demanded.

Neil rolled his eyes and scooped up a handful of cheese. "Well, who else has an uncle who could afford to buy two hundred buttons? Makes it a lot easier, doesn't it?"

"Neil, what are you talking about?"

"Mandy's father is some big airline pilot, right?" Neil asked.

I nodded.

"Yeah, well he bought two hundred bucks worth of your buttons tonight at the last minute."

"Uncle Olas?" I asked, as if my plate would answer.

"Mandy said she didn't want to tell me that," Neil added. "She only did because the 4-H should be aware of her father's

contribution, though she said he always refuses acknowledge-
ment for his generosity."

Humiliation is a strange sensation. It doesn't feel like a swarm of
wasps in your head until after it bucks you in the stomach. I left my
loaded plate on the buffet table and fled to my father. He drove me
home, no questions asked, and as I got out of the car I insisted, "I'll
be out in the barn and I don't want anybody to call me in."

It wasn't easy climbing over the pen rails with my puffball
dress. The twin lambs raised sleepy heads to witness my struggle.
They remained curled in the straw near each other and I crowded
up against them, their soft woolly curls in my face, a hard little
hoof dug into my shin, their lanolin smell in my nostrils. My
tears didn't penetrate their coats.

I heard the other cars arrive in the driveway. My heart stopped
each time, wondering if it was Neil coming to beg forgiveness. I
heard my brothers and mother, and later, Mandy and her parents.

A car door slammed and Uncle Olas' raised voice penetrated the
barn walls. His words were slurred, "And don't think the s-s-silent
treatment will work, Mandy! I say it again, that was a disgusk-k—a
disgusting shock to see you in that boy's truck like that!"

"Olas, please keep your voice down," Aunt Eileen pleaded.
She sounded plaintive, lacking her earlier enthusiasm. "You're
upset about nothing. A harmless kiss or two."

Mandy's voice was level and calculated, "Get used to it, Daddy.
I'm very pretty and boys want me now. Anyway, in this case I was
only offering the boy some sympathy. Camille dumped him."

Aunt Eileen's voice went up an octave, "That was Cammie's
boyfriend?"

"Yes," Mandy said. "She gets named Queen and proceeds to
ignore him."

"Really?" Aunt Eileen said with disgust.

Uncle Olas said, "Well, then I'm sorry I spent a lousy two
bucks-s on the little bitch's button!"

My hand stroked the lambs' backs. One of them stood up, tot-
tered away from me, lay back down. "Liar!" I was repeating in my
head. "Liar!" I stayed there in the straw.

It was near dawn before I went into the house. Shivering, I crossed the yard with its damp air and coat of heavy dew, my way lit by the tight, thin lip of light on the horizon. Inside, the only sound was Uncle Olas' snoring. Mandy was asleep in my bed, her hair spread out around her in haloed glory. The sheep shears felt cold and heavy in my hand. I made one quick buzzing pass over Mandy's scalp before she woke up, felt the bald patch with a languid, sleepy hand, and started to scream.

Angel Cravings

MIRABETH GRIPPED THE ENDS OF THE WISHBONE FROM THE holiday turkey with her pinkie fingers, closed her eyes, assigned two wishes—a right-hand wish and a left-hand wish—and snapped the bone. When she opened her eyes, her left pinkie held the prize of the knobby piece. She sighed and tossed the frail splinters onto the table. Had one of her wishes ever been fulfilled? Did it matter which end of the wishbone won? Maybe if she'd had more birthday candles to blow out when she was little, but Aunt Adeline had only ever managed to remember her birthday twice.

Mirabeth ripped the drumstick off the carcass and frowned at it. The women's magazines she stocked at the library wagged their fingers at late-night snacking: not a healthy lifestyle choice. Mirabeth hesitated a moment—focused on the meat, its enticing leftovers' aroma—then she became distracted by the sporadic twitch in her right eye as it tugged at her eyelid. A sure sign that she shouldn't be up so late. Blinking hard, she bit into the drumstick and, with greasy fingers, reached over to switch off the

97

kitchen light in the hope it would help relieve her twitch.

At the moment the room was plunged into darkness, Mirabeth looked out the kitchen window and saw what looked like a halo rising up above the street lamp. She blinked hard, thinking maybe it was her twitch, but she continued to see it rise into the darkness, illuminating the softly falling midnight snowflakes as it passed upwards. There was a second ascending halo, then a third, and then they vanished. A voluminous sense of awe filled Mirabeth. And with a sudden insight, both pure and rare, the notion of an angel exodus struck her—came with such clarity, she began to choke on her mouthful of holiday turkey.

It took several hard hacks before the meat dislodged from her throat. She continued to hold her breath afterwards, listening for Lloyd down the hall in the bedroom, for the steadiness of his snore. She couldn't risk waking him at that moment! The silence roared at her, she listened so hard. Then she heard it: the light, snuffling nasal intake, the loose exhalation. She relaxed, took her own deep breath, and wondered why women sought relief from partners who snored. She found the sound of Lloyd's measured zeds more calming than any lavender aromatherapy. She had learned, however, in the short time since he'd moved into her house, just how easily his rasping rhythms could be interrupted. Lloyd, nearly forty, two hundred and twenty pounds, still seemed to be afraid of the dark; some bogey-man threat made him a light and needy sleeper. Spooners was his preferred bedtime position, his loins pressed into Mirabeth's bottom, his thick arm wrapped around her. This, not his snoring, was what kept her awake, thinking about fireflies in mason jars, chained dogs, and snow-shoe rabbits in trap-line snares—she not being accustomed to sharing a bed with anyone.

The kitchen clock ticked. Lloyd's snore maintained its peaceful steadiness. She turned on the kitchen light and tiptoed to the fridge. She had discovered also that he slept most soundly for one hour after sex. That meant she could count on a half-hour more. She removed the jellied salad, jabbed a spoon into it and shoved a large wedge into her mouth. She held its slippery coldness against her tongue for a moment and realized she was going to need more than a half-hour to sort out her revelation. All the angels leaving!? The archangels and the lowlier ones; angels that could hold up a corner of the earth and the ministering ones; and especially the white ones with wings and a glow—those she imagined most often. What a ridiculous thought, but there it was—augered into her head. Inescapable! The world had spent the past year wildly debating what the end of the millennium would bring to mankind, and she had just been offered an insight.

She tried to recall all that she'd read over the past year: everything from apocalyptic religion to the Y2K bug. But of what she could remember, angels didn't figure that heavily into any of it; except for the occasional reference to them with their trumpets and vials contributing to the demise of the world. No one, anywhere, had mentioned that the dawn of the year 2000 was the date the angels' lease ran out. They had to go! And they had to go far: to another universe to make room for the millions and millions of the next ten centuries' dead. The angels out of reach, out of touch? That could create a chaos far more threatening than any computer glitch, Mirabeth determined.

Her bare arms tightened into a mass of goosebumps, and she heard Lloyd, down the hall, mumble aloud in his sleep. She hoped he wasn't having nightmares about his kids, who lived hundreds of miles away in Winnipeg with his ex-wife. She wanted to go and look in on him, but she had to deal with her revelation, and besides, she was still ravenous. Sex did that to her and she had spent most of her life unaware of it. She was thankful to Lloyd for having changed that, though she had never admitted to him that something about the way he had lumbered into the library after his divorce, seeking solace in free books, had awakened her sexual urges from a near-death dormancy. No, not something she could easily tell him: at times, he seemed more shy in bed than she herself.

Her gooseflesh convinced her that cold jelly salad was unappealing. She put two slices of bread into the toaster for something warm, then remembered the cranberry sauce. Cold or not, she ladled it onto the toast and bit in. It tasted of holidays past. It tasted of Aunt Adeline's house: a hint of mustiness, vaguely astringent. Mirabeth had come to avoid thinking of her spinster aunt since the older woman's death a decade earlier, but something about the cranberries caused Mirabeth to recall the day she had fallen out of Aunt Adeline's gnarled crabapple tree. It had been the only time that Mirabeth had ever heard her legal guardian shriek, had ever seen her run out of the house to kneel on the grass.

Aunt Adeline had said, in short, sharp, winded breaths, her chin high in the air as she had looked down her nose and felt for bumps on Mirabeth's head, "You must have a guardian angel looking after you, child."

Mirabeth had taken advantage of the moment, of Aunt Adeline's unexpected show of concern. She had swallowed her sniffles and asked, "Do you think if my mother had had a guardian angel that she would have drowned at the floodway, Auntie Adeline?"

The older woman had sucked in her cheeks. "Oh, look here, you have a bruise on your arm," she had replied.

"That was there before I fell out of the tree," Mirabeth had stated then pressed on, "She mustn't have had one, do you think?"

"Perhaps she wore out her guardian angel," Aunt Adeline had said and tilted her chin a degree higher. "Perhaps Gabby's—your mother's—guardian angel was taking a personal day, the way they allow your teachers to do now. Since she was my baby sister and your Nanny Patterson insisted I take care of her much of the time, I can speak with authority when I say that I'm sure your mother could tire out an angel. She had a way of finding trouble."

Aunt Adeline had lifted Mirabeth to her feet, then started back to the house. Mirabeth skip-limped behind her, following her inside, continuing to chatter.

"I don't remember her getting into trouble, but then sometimes I wonder if I remember her at all or if I just make up what I remember. Maybe I'll ask Nanny Patterson next time we visit her at the farm. Like, I think I remember my mother leaning over my bed—my bed was right under the window and the curtains had little dots on gauzy see-through kind of fabric—and she would kiss me goodnight; but maybe I'm just making that up in my head because that's what I want to remember. How do I know for sure my mother really did that? I was only four, you know?"

Aunt Adeline's ramrod back had slumped then and her chin fell to her chest making her look like a tired comma, and she had said, as if she were speaking to her flat stomach and no one else, "I know you were only four. I know the exact date you came to live here. Now, you don't have a concussion so go back outside to play! And don't court any more trouble. You don't want to wear out your guardian angel, Mirabeth, do you?"

"But, how do you know, Auntie Adeline, for sure about guardian angels?" Mirabeth had called the words from the screen door, her nose pressed against it so that she could smell the sharp scent of dusty metal.

"I read it in a book," had been Aunt Adeline's reply. And although Mirabeth had never witnessed her aunt actually reading a book, she had known it must be so; after all, at the time, Aunt Adeline had been the head librarian in Nakitoka Lake.

Mirabeth licked her finger, dotted up the toast crumbs on her kitchen table, popped them into her mouth. She looked out the window, searching for a sign of other ascending halos. It was starting to snow harder. The forecast was for heavy accumulations of snow over the next twenty-four hours. How often had it snowed, really snowed, on December 31st, Mirabeth pondered? Not very often. It was normally cold and clear. But then, how often did the calendar change over to a new millennium? Mirabeth squinted and thought the snow looked like a multitude of angel feathers falling to earth. Perhaps the angels were experiencing a massive moult before growing the new wings that would carry them to the next universe. And where did this angel exodus leave her? Without a guardian angel—that's where. It would leave everyone who had one, without one. A few angels would remain nearby, she decided: the cherubim that He placed to guard the east end of Eden after He banished Adam and Eve would still be around. Notice, Mirabeth thought, how there were no cherubim or angels to guard them before the fact. Why not? Why didn't any of those Psalm's angels make an earlier appearance to keep charge over Eve lest she dash her foot against a stone or lest she meet up with some twisted serpent? Mirabeth figured that Eve herself, after her death, must have been the first guardian-type angel. Who would know better than Eve about the perils of making the wrong choice? Who else would accept the responsibility of protecting her daughters—women with no identities, and no alternatives than to marry their own brothers? Which meant, Mirabeth figured, that sinners didn't go to hell: they were designated as guardian angels and given awesome responsibilities instead. No wonder there was a celestial overcrowding problem, and He, being an all-or-nothing kind of Guy, and with all Infinity to choose from, was clearing the guardian angels out *en masse* at the millennium's end…not worrying about continuity, just shipping them off. Angel refugees. Mirabeth concluded that the predictions of millennium doom might well come true, at least until the guardian angel stocks could be replenished. And was she, in some way, responsible for the world, having been given the knowledge of the imminent angel exodus? Mirabeth's eye twitched. She rummaged through the refrigerator, found the gherkins, speared several out of their narrow jar, and reasoned that if He had wanted the world to know, He would have cued some TV evangelist or news reporter, not a librarian in Nakitoka Lake. No, Mirabeth decided, it was a personal revelation with which she was dealing, and she had to ponder for herself what to make of it.

She tiptoed to the back hall closet and buttoned her winter coat over top of her flimsy nightie. She had the need to feel the snowflakes—to know if they would melt in her palm or remain there, causing her to giggle or sneeze. She wondered if a person could be allergic to angel feathers?

Maybe that's what ailed Lloyd's daughter, Caitlin, who had several allergies, she thought. But no, after having met Lloyd's kids, Caitlin and Jeremy, for the first time the previous summer, Mirabeth had decided that the unfortunate pair were devoid of any other-worldly contacts. There especially weren't any angels hovering around Caitlin. Her lip and eyebrow rings, her tongue stud seemed strategically placed to ward them off. Mirabeth had thought this to herself on the day they were crammed onto their towels at Grand Beach, under a cloud-plagued sky, watching Lloyd wave and salute to them as he inched his shins into Lake Winnipeg.

Mirabeth was used to kids, preferring to hang out in the children's stacks whenever she could sneak away from her administrative duties. In fact, she had started working in the children's section back when Aunt Adeline had been in charge of the library. Kids seemed to like Mirabeth, particularly when she performed dramatic readings of *Peter Pan* and *Gulliver's Travels*. But the situation with Lloyd's children baffled her. She couldn't play town librarian with them, and she was just learning the role of Lloyd's girlfriend herself; performing it for such a critical audience was a lot to ask. The best she could do was avoid irritating them and hope that someday they might come to accept her. Lloyd was no help. When he lay on the beach between his children, Mirabeth could almost see the Lilliputian ropes crisscrossed over his chest and down the length of his body, each little strand representing some aspect of his children's lives that had become incomprehensible to him. A strand here for how Caitlin had learned, since the divorce, to strum his old guitar and sing tunes in an off-key wail; a strand there for the way Jeremy punctuated every one of Lloyd's enthusiastic suggestions with, *That's gonna suck*. Lloyd had tried to struggle against the ropes (by doing things like spending Christmas in a downtown Winnipeg hotel so he could be with his children over the holidays and not uproot them from their own Christmas tree), but Mirabeth believed that distance and time were strengthening the tethers and it was becoming increasingly more difficult for Lloyd to embrace Caitlin and Jeremy with his arms bound against his sides.

When Mirabeth stepped outdoors, her feet bare inside her winter boots, the air was weighted with snow. She stuck her tongue out and caught a multitude of flakes that disappeared into a wet nothingness in her mouth. Not angel feathers, after all. Or perhaps angel feathers melt in your mouth too. If she had never before attempted to eat an angel, how would she know? Mirabeth's bare knees were cold. She squatted down in the snow and covered them with the length of her coat. She could have been praying there with her hands clasped under her chin.

"Mirabeth, what are you doing outside?" She heard Lloyd's voice behind her at the back door. "I woke up and couldn't find you," he added. "Scared the hell out of me."

"So, you couldn't sleep then, Lloyd?" Mirabeth said from her squatting position, her words let out in a visible puff in the winter air.

"Hang on a second, I'll grab my coat," she heard him say. He always responded with a physical action at the slightest hint of disappointment in her voice. Sometimes Lloyd reminded her of Nanny Patterson in that way. The few times Mirabeth had visited her grandmother's farm with Aunt Adeline, Nanny Patterson had responded to everything that Mirabeth said or did with some course of action: a walk to the cookie jar, a wipe with a tissue, a hauling out of photo albums from old suitcases, a squeezing of lemons to make lemonade, a kiss on a scratched knee.

Mirabeth had said to her one day, "Auntie Adeline says that I must have a guardian angel, Nanny. Do you believe that?"

"Yes, yes, oh yes I do," Nanny Patterson had replied and patted Mirabeth on the head.

"If I have a guardian angel, then why did my mother drown?"

Nanny Patterson's bottom lip had pumped up and down as if it had to be primed to find a response, "Well," she had said with a sputter, "your mother—my precious Gabby—must be your guardian angel, Mirabeth! There was no sense, no sense in it, in her being taken so young, otherwise."

Nanny had hoisted herself off the sofa, retrieved her sweater from the dining room chair and wrapped it around Mirabeth's shoulders. "And someday, someday," she had continued, "but not for a long while yet, you'll be together with your mother in heaven. In the meantime, she looks out for you everyday; of that, I'm sure, positive, haven't a doubt in my mind about that.

"As a matter of fact, you know how sometimes when you're sitting alone in a room, and out of the corner of your eye you see a flicker of someone there? Well that's your guardian angel. Or, you're writing a math test and the question looks like Greek, then all of a sudden, the answer is whispered into your brain? Or when you're about to trip down the stairs, but you regain your balance and your heart is thumping because you don't know how you managed to keep from going ass-over-tea-kettle? Well that's your guardian angel—your mother—at work. Of that I'm certain, absolutely," Nanny had said with a definite nod.

It was Lloyd's large hands on her shoulders that stopped Mirabeth's thoughts from running on about Nanny Patterson. He said, "You're starting to look like a snowman out here," and brushed the large flakes from her coat and her hair.

"You know, Lloyd," Mirabeth reflected, "I've spent my whole life wishing that I could have my mother back. When I was a kid, I believed that if I wished hard enough, it would happen. When I grew up a little and realized it wouldn't, I put my faith in the idea that when I died, I'd be reunited with her; but as of tonight, I realize there are no guarantees."

Lloyd stopped brushing at the snow and, down on his knees beside Mirabeth, he kept perfectly still.

The snow started to cover the two of them; a light layer of whiteness; the odd flake catching in their eyelashes, blinked away.

"What makes you think that?" Lloyd asked after a long pause. "It says in the newspapers that people are finding their faith for the new millennium, not losing it."

"I don't know if it's a loss of faith, Lloyd, maybe just a rerouting caused by one of those insights that forces you to stop feeling sorry for yourself. Don't they refer to that as maturity on those phone-in talk radio shows?"

Lloyd chuckled. He started to brush the snow off Mirabeth again. "Hey," he stated, "if you don't get some sleep now you

won't be able to stay up long enough tonight to ring in the new millennium. You won't know if the hydro goes off or anything!"
Mirabeth looked at her watch. It was almost 2:00 a.m.

"You know, Lloyd," she continued, "the year 2000 would be an excellent one in which to bear a child. No new millennium change-over lurking for a full thousand more years. Strangely comforting, that thought, being able to stick around . . ." her words trailed off and mingled with the snowflakes.

Lloyd stared at her, his forehead wrinkled. Mirabeth avoided his confused look and gazed up into the sky. He looked up too, way up overhead, and his vocal chords seemed stretched when he said, "Is this some odd way of telling me that you want to have a baby, Mirabeth?" He looked at her again, surrounded her with his bulky arms, held her face tightly against the front of his parka.

Mirabeth didn't struggle; she let his warmth sink into her body, while she thought about her left-hand wishbone wish. You couldn't tell anyone your wish or it wouldn't come true, isn't that what Nanny Patterson had once stated?

She said to Lloyd, "I have a craving right now for a big piece of cake. Angel food. Why do people crave what they don't have?"

"There's that whole fruit cake that Caitlin and Jeremy gave me for Christmas," Lloyd suggested.

They went back into the house, ate thick slabs of the fruit-filled cake at the kitchen table, watched the snowfall taper off, and much later, gazing out the bedroom window, Mirabeth and Lloyd sampled the first slice of dawn as it sweetened the last day of the millennium.

Fire-Eater

"GO GIRL, PEEL AND FLING NOW, DARLIA-DANCER, YOU PRANCER, you take-a-chancer, you fire necromancer!" That's what I'm chanting in my head as the most exotic of the exotic dancers ever to come to the Hematite Hotel is doing her fire-eating striptease; even though I'm pissed off at Lenny, who hasn't taken his eyes off her since she took the stage. He's war-whooped, licked his lips, sucked the last ice cube out of his rye and seven like he's been going desperate for a year without any. I want to grab one of Darlia-dancer's flaming swords and stab him in the heart. The son-of-a-bitch. What's his problem anyway? What are any of their problems? I look around the smoke-clogged barroom. There's almost as many women here—what else is there to do on a Friday night in Hematite besides go to the one movie theatre and watch a movie where you can't understand a word they're speaking because the sound system was installed during the silent-picture era and everyone constantly interrupts the movie, shouting "Turn it up"? It doesn't turn up! If it did, you'd only be cranking up distorted static. It sounds like air-traffic controllers talking when the lovers argue, kiss and make up. Forget the machine-gun-fire movies, you go home with a headache ... that's when Lenny doesn't get any! But I forgot what I started out to say, and that is, that all the men in the bar tonight are mesmerized by Darlia, this mocha-skinned majesty of a flame-swallowing stripper, and so are most of the women. And I'd probably be enjoying her a lot more if I hadn't had too much to drink and wasn't in the mood to take a few swings at Lenny. I want to pummel him for not wanting to get engaged and legitimize this relationship. "Too many rocks around this town already!" he said again tonight when I started hinting about a ring. He offered to bring me a nice big, round, iron ore pellet from the processing plant where he's in charge of making sure the conveyor belts don't break down. Sleeps half of his shifts away—I'm sure of it—Lenny is not what you'd call an enthusiastic worker, but he has his good points. He's fun, Lenny is! Whenever he jokes about stuff like engagement rings, he snaps back his head and roars at his own sense of humour, and even though I hate his comments, his laugh is infectious. It starts my toes wriggling. I can't help that: I'm a sucker for a guy who can make me laugh. I have to do something to steel myself against that. Yeah, I have to admit that my being pissed-off has very little to do with Darlia-the-Dancer or her African-drummer accompanist. Listen to the big words that run through my head when I'm drunk. Out loud, I've never spoken the words "accompanist" or "infectious" or "legitimize." Are those words? Repeating them in my head, I'm getting the feeling they're not words.

I slip into the bathroom. It's hotter in here than in the beverage room. Air-conditioner is always breaking down in the Hematite Hotel. There's no one else in the bathroom because they're all glued to their seats by the extra heat that Dancing Darlia and her edible flames are producing, so I can talk to the mirror freely. I've learned to gauge how drunk I am by the time-lapse between what I'm saying out loud and how it comes back to me in the mirror. I can never synchronize the two when I'm really drunk, but if I'm just a bit tipsy, I can concentrate hard and

get the two to line up. Tonight, I'm the tortoise and the hare—
two different speeds—but can you believe I used the word "syn-
chronize"? I should stay drunk all the time, not just Friday
nights. I'd come off a lot smarter and maybe they'd make me
manager at the store, instead of shipping and receiving clerk. I
wonder if I'd get pricked by any more fish hooks if I became
manager? I bet I'd never have to count fish hooks again, and if I
did, I'd hire someone else to do it because I'd be the manager!
And what the hell does the word "necromancer" mean? That just
popped into my head when I was making my rhyme. I like
rhymes. I've always liked rhymes. What's that supposed to say
about me? I'd make a great rhyming store manager. Not too
much call for that in Hematite. I wonder if somewhere they offer
free world cruises for people who like to rhyme?

When I walk out of the bathroom, I see Hans Rousseau, the
hunkiest of the hunks of the whole goddamn town, walking up
towards the stage. He's weaving ever so slightly. Hans is usually
too busy making moves on the dance floor to get drunk, but
because of Darlia the fire-eater, there's no live band this weekend.
She's doing two shows nightly. No dancing for the rest of us, so
Hans is having a little trouble negotiating his way up there. Don't
you love that? "Negotiating"? Ha! I'm a fucking genius!

It all happens so fast, it's like some kind of dream sequence,
but Hans is up there with his glass of draught beer and he pours
it on Darlia's big bowl of fire-lighting coals. There's a huge gasp
in the place. I wait for the giant fire ball to explode—he's pouring
alcohol on fire, for chrissakes! (I do remember a little high school
chemistry.) But nothing happens! Just this hissing sizzle and a lit-
tle puff of smoke and then a split-second eerie silence before
Darlia screeches, and her African-drumming accompanist (who
is like the biggest black man anyone in this town has ever seen
because we have no people of that ancestry living here), jumps
over his congas, grabs hold of Hans and throws him up against
the wall. The walls inside the Hematite Hotel are brick. Hardly a
goddamn brick on the outside of any houses in this town, except
Doc Chrysler's house, because mostly every house was built

within a two-year span to meet the demands of the huge influx of men who came to work the Hematite Mine. Mine opens, gotta have men. Men gotta have houses. Men gotta have wives or else you gotta have a whole hell of a lot of working ladies. And men gotta have something to spend their money on other than booze and poker, so they gotta have kids—kids'll suck you dry, money-wise. Mostly this town has tiny little houses, barely room for all the kids. Wood and stucco. But inside the Hematite Hotel there's brick. Go figure.

I imagine it hurts the back of Hans' head when the accompanist shoves him up there, then drives his fist into Hans' guts a couple of times. Ol' Macaffrey, who was behind the bar, shoots out faster than a snake's tongue to make sure none of his glasses get broken or tables busted up. He helps the accompanist drag Hans to the door and throw him out, to the cheers of the crowd. Me, I don't cheer. I start bawling. Go figure. I hate violence, really. Scares the hell out of me when two assholes start going at each other. It happens every Friday night. If not the men, then once in a while, the women start it up. And even though I talk big, I've never so much as slapped Lenny's face, though he's deserved it how many times? That's another good thing about Lenny: he never manhandles me, and he doesn't rumble it up in macho matches. Lenny is well-liked. No one, except a moron, would pick a fight with him. And if one did, then a whole crew of guys would rally together to put the boots to the moron, so Lenny would never have to fight him alone.

I go back inside the ladies' room and lock myself in a stall for a few minutes. Long enough for Lenny to wonder where the hell I've gotten to. I imagine everybody out there talking all at once about what just happened, then Lenny looking to make some joke about it to me, and me not there and him scratching his head as to why not. That gets me thinking, which is always a danger-ous thing when I've had too much to drink. Don't think, Monica Marshmallow-head, don't think. But I can't help myself. For the hundredth time, I think about using some of my savings to buy my own ring and tell everyone that Lenny gave it to me. Then I think, I don't want to go home with Lenny tonight. Not now. Not ever. That kind of thought can send you puking in the toilet, which is precisely what happens next, because that kind of thought sends a whole range of nervous agitation into your stomach region. At one end of the range, you've got this incredible feeling of power and a sense of freedom so fat, it's as if you could fly out the Hematite Hotel door; but at the other end you're scared shitless. If not Lenny, then what? What emptiness? Anything, even Lenny, is better than lonely all the time. Isn't it?

I rinse my mouth out a dozen times and chew up a couple of Chiclets to kill the rancid bitterness. I splash some water on my face, icy cold, and dry it with the scratchy, brown, piece of paper towel. Feels better. I look like crap. I go straight for the back door, behind Ol' Macaffrey's bar. He's still up at the stage, trying to apologize to Darlia for the mishap. I take one last look at the back of Lenny's head and I'm out of there, through the stock room piled high with beer cases and Smirnoff boxes, and out under the red glowing Exit sign into the back alley behind the Hematite Hotel.

I take a minute and breathe in the summer evening. Even with the dumpsters out back, it smells so goddamn fresh after the smoke and stale-beer-spilled-in-the-carpet smell of the Hematite. That's when I see Hans. He's lying on his back on the still-warm asphalt, coughing a little, one arm flung over his gut as if he's keeping it there to fend off any other fists that might come looking for his mid-section. There's a bare bulb over the door I've just come out of, and there's still a haze of light on the horizon, making black silhouettes of the pine trees across the river. The Hematite Hotel has the best view of the river, even from the alleyway. Prime land is what the Hematite Hotel sits on, but who would ever know it? Most everyone coming out of there is too drunk to see.

I walk towards him really slowly. "Hey, Hans," I say.

He blinks hard a couple of times. Maybe he was crying and he's trying to clear the tears, so I keep my distance, but he turns his head and smiles up at me.

"Hey, Monica." He props himself up on his elbow and says, "I was just taking a little nap."

Another wisecracker, I think, but I smile back anyway, because I suspected Hans wouldn't even remember my name. He was a couple of years ahead of me in high school and dated girls that moved in different social circles from me. Girls with tighter pants, girls that knew how to apply eyeliner in a steady line before they even had their periods. I've discovered since then there's nothing much to that. I can probably apply straight eyeliner in my sleep now, but back then I was intimidated by simple things.

"Are you okay?" I ask, and my voice is too high and tight and it echoes back at me off the walls and garbage bins.

"Just peachy," he answers, kind of mimicking my voice, and I have to smile again because it sounds so lame.

"Can you get up? I could help you to your truck or something."

"No," Hans says and he flashes me a really big smile when he adds, "I'm avoiding the parking lot right now. I don't think the paying customers appreciated my fire-safety training."

I laugh right out loud this time. I forgot that Hans works for Natural Resources, co-ordinating fire-fighting crews. A fire boss.

"Ah!" I say. "So with all the rain this summer, you had to go looking for work?"

It's Hans' turn to laugh. He holds his gut when he does and responds, "Something like that." He gets to his feet, takes a deep breath. "Remind me never to fight a guy who beats a drum with his bare hands for a living. There's real power in their punches."

I lean a little closer in case he falls back down, but he straightens his back and sniffs.

He's not quite as gorgeous as I remember him from high school. Although he still has those startling, bright blue eyes, there's a few worry lines around them and his hairline is receding just a fraction. But, he's got a gorgeous tan and a pretty much perfect body.

I stand there with nothing to say, but Hans is a smooth-talker.

He leans against the wall with one hand and starts in, "So, some of the summer recruits were up at the store this week for hatchets and maps, told me that a *real honey* filled their order. I told them, *Must have been Monica*. Was I right?"

I nod. He knows where I work, too. Why should that make me feel as if there's something warm kindling inside me? I keep my eyes focused on the river.

"So, Monica, what are you doing out here without Lenny?"

I shrug and turn away; pretend I can't take my eyes off the view of the river. The last of the dusk light is fading from the pines. In a moment you won't see the tree line any longer. When I turn back to look at Hans, I see the moths starting to congregate around the bare bulb behind his head. He kicks at some loose gravel with his hiking boots, and says, "So, do you want to grab a cup of coffee?"

"I could use coffee," I say. "Do we chance the parking lot?"

"No," he says. "Let's walk down to Parkie's."

"Okay," I say. "Shortcut?"

He nods.

Though the path won't be lit, I guess anybody who grew up in Hematite could find their way to Parkie's in the dark using the shortcut along the river bank and up over the outcropping of rock where the town curfew siren stands. It's the same path where everybody gets their first kiss, their first feel-up, probably lots have acquired more than that off the trail a bit, though I've never been one to enjoy doing it with the rugged spine of the Canadian Shield sticking in my back.

Down at the river's edge, it feels cooler. The path is soggy from all the rain we've been having. It squishes up around my sandals, but I don't care—even though they're new and I bought them in Thunder Bay, full price—because there's something so sublime about the smell of damp soil and willow bushes mixed with Hans' aftershave. The cool ooze seeping in around my feet makes me shiver. When I slip on a mossy rock, Hans' arm is lightning fast and catches my waist to keep me from going down. I guess a couple punches in the gut sober a guy up pretty fast, but maybe not fast enough, because he pulls me towards his chest and I feel my heart thumping against his flannel shirt. Only men who work for Natural Resources wear flannel shirts in the heat of summer, I'm thinking to myself, when his lips come down on mine ever so gentle, roving there, picking up momentum, making my head buzz as if there's a water-bomber overhead. For a long couple of minutes I can't fucking think of one big word!

After we start back down the trail, the word *womanizer* pops in. That's fairly big, but not impressively so. I must be sobering up. I think of all the women I've seen Hans Rousseau with and I lose count fairly quickly. Lots of them I haven't even known: Out-of-towners. Locals. Tourists. Even female ecology majors from the southern Ontario universities, recruited to fight fires for the summer...too young to be messing with the likes of Hans Rousseau. He woos them all. *Hans Never-Solo* is what the locals call him. He is not discerning. Chrissakes, he just kissed me. Discerning—there's another word I've never spoken out loud before. Maybe I am still under the influence.

Parkie's is quiet when we finally arrive there. I'm still tingling on the spots where Hans' hands roved up under my shirt. We sit at a booth in the back and the owner, Sherilee, raises her eyebrow at me when she pours out two coffees. Hans tells Sherilee she's looking good on Friday night and she flashes her false teeth at him, smoothes her uniform over her hips.

"Thanks for the big tip last week," she says.

He responds, "Hey, best coffee this side of the Arctic Circle. That's what I tell everybody."

For some reason their prattle is annoying me. I dump two teaspoonfuls of sugar into my coffee and add two creamers before I stir. Hans turns his attention back to me; flicks his head in the direction of Sherilee and gives me a wink. Like we're co-conspirators, he whispers, "She'll make a fresh pot now and our refills will be free."

"She can't make any money that way," I lean forward to say.

Hans runs his finger down the bridge of my nose and stops on the tip giving it a little tap. He answers, "Natural Resources boys eat here enough to keep Sherilee in trips to Vegas every winter. Don't sweat it."

For no good reason, I want to swat at his finger, but then he winces when he reaches further forward over the table to cup my hand and he gets the better of me.

I say, "Maybe you should see Doc Chrysler?"

"Naw, I'll just have a big nasty bruise in the morning. Nothing I can't handle. It'll be like I spent the night with some wild woman."

I grimace, then say, "So why'd you do it?"

"Do what?"

"Pour your beer over her coals?"

Hans picks up his coffee and drinks. Avoids my eyes.

"You a bigot or something?"

He practically chokes on his coffee. "Is that what you think? That I'm prejudiced against women of colour? Holy shit." He looks at me like I'm a moron.

My toes are cold now. The air-conditioner at Parkie's is always on full blast. I put my hands around my coffee cup and hold the steam to my face.

He sighs, rubs his free hand across his chin. I hear the bristles rasp. I want to reach over and make that sound, too.

He says, "I think I just sort of freaked, is all."

"What?!"

"Too many tequilas before I switched to beer!" he says, forcing a laugh, then his face folds in again, and he confides, "Some kind of flashback thing happening with the heat in there." He sounds sheepish enough that I wonder if maybe he's not bullshitting me.

"No way," I mutter.

Hans stares at me, then says, "Hey, you doubt my job is dangerous? You think I fall asleep at night and don't have nightmares about sending eighteen-year-old kids to dig at the edge of an approaching out-of-control to try to contain it? You ever been battling the blaze in front of you when the wind shifts and gusts, shifts and gusts, and the next thing you know it's an inferno roaring in every fucking direction you can turn?" Hans' voice is getting louder and Sherilee stretches her neck from her *National Enquirer* to see what the fuss is about.

I pat his hand. "Hey, Hans . . . it's okay . . . it's okay."

" . . . Yeah, and when I've risked enough lives all summer to save another forest or two, the other half of this town comes along the following winter and chops and skids it away to the pulp and paper mill! Don't you ever wonder what you're doing with your life, Monica? Don't you get tired of . . . of what? . . . of unpacking fishing lures for a living so some American tourist can leave them on a log at the bottom of a lake? Don't you ever want the water to wash it all away? Don't you just want to douse something and follow the rivulets of water down the path of least resistance?" He's not shouting anymore. He's leaned over the table, but his quiet words are more intense than if he'd had a megaphone. It's almost as if I can hear a crackling sound coming off of him combined with a whiff of smoke.

I guess that's why neither of us notices that Lenny and two of his buddies are standing six feet away from our table, until Lenny says my name. I let go of Hans' hand as I whirl around, rattling the coffee cups on the table.

Hans leans back and says, "Hey, guys!" He makes it sound all innocent and like nothing's up, but I can see the veins on Lenny's neck bulging out like I've never seen them before.

Lenny says, "What the hell are you doing here, Monica?" His friends are standing back, shifting their weight from one foot to the other, trying to avoid looking at me.

"Kinda hard to explain," I say. "One second I'm puking in the bathroom, and the next I'm out in the alley gulping air and I find Hans here doing the same thing." I don't know if Lenny believes me, because I'm too busy listening to myself, listening to the quaver in my voice that sounds guilty and void of big words. Void, that's a nice word. I try it out. "I should have said, I was voiding, not puking. Or does that mean something else? Yeah, *voiding* would not be used correctly there," is what I add to my explanation.

"You trying to make me look like an asshole in front of my friends, Monica?" Lenny says.

"Hey," Hans interrupts. "No sweat, man. We were just having a cup of coffee. We both needed a cup of coffee. Different reasons. That's all."

It's like some kind of déjà vu, or something. All of a sudden, Lenny and his two buddies are dragging Hans out of the booth and through the door. This time, it's my voice that's shrieking! Sherilee is right behind us screaming that she's gonna call the cops, but Lenny and his buddies don't listen. Two of them continue to hold onto Hans while Lenny takes a swing at him. He misses. Hans shakes off Lenny's buddies, and it turns out they're scared shitless because in the next breath, the pair of them are hightailing it out of there. Hans and Lenny are left to square off alone on the sidewalk outside Parkie's. The Friday-night-cruising traffic is slowing down to see what's going on. Hans raises his arms indicating he's willing to forget about the whole thing right now, but Lenny calls him an asshole and rushes at him. A single punch from Hans drops Lenny to the pavement. Hans is preparing to haul him up and hit him a second time, but I scream again. Hans stops and looks at me. Lenny's lip is cut and the top of his cheekbone is starting to swell shut over his eye.

Hans is breathing hard as he takes a step away from Lenny and closer to me, steadies himself before he speaks. It's like he's begging me for something when he says, "Monica, please tell me if there's been enough fire-eating for one night?"

I lean towards Hans' outstretched hand. In my head there's a ridiculous rhyme, "Monica, Monica, what do you wantica?" I can't understand what the words from Hans' question mean. I'm not sure if they're moving too fast or too slow. But I know somewhere in the dictionary, there's a definition for what I'm about to do.

Indebted

KEITH SPRAWLS ON THE CHINTZ SOFA, WEARING NOTHING BUT A thick, white guest towel. The skin on his freckled shoulders has been peeling since their second day here. Meg hopes the towel is not wet but says nothing; she has bigger concerns.

He grumbles, "Can't we just stay put this evening? Beg off with a headache?"

Stage-whispering back, trying not to raise her voice because the guest cottage stands only thirty-five feet off the glass-walled main house and she doesn't want the Lannets to hear them arguing, she says, "Honey, we're obligated to Art and Yolanda!"

"Meg," Keith retorts, "I'm tired of feeling obligated to the Lannets. I didn't want us to come on this trip. Bad idea, I said, remember?"

She slips the new seashell bracelet Keith bought her from a trinket stand that afternoon onto her wrist, and tries to reason with him. "Keith, how can you be so ungrateful? Look around you . . . this is not frozen prairie! Sunshine. Ocean. We could never have afforded this on our own . . . even though business has doubled over the past two years . . . thanks to Art and Yolanda."

He stands, grabbing at the towel to keep it from slipping off. With his free hand, he opens the bar fridge and mixes himself a rum and Coke.

"Oh, a drink's going to help," Meg mutters.

Keith shoots Meg a look and doesn't respond until he's downed half of it. Some of the dark liquid slops onto the counter top when he smacks the glass down. Meg hustles over, wets a cloth, wipes the spill, wrings out the cloth, wets it again, and wipes a second time to ensure there's nothing left behind.

Unwrapping the edge of the towel he's wearing, Keith dries the spot, then he sighs. "Meg, you know I was appreciative when Art hired me to cater the meals on their movie set; and I was grateful when Yolanda recommended us to other local producers. And hey! I was as delighted as you when they arranged those music lessons for Janie . . . and the piano deal . . . baby grand and all. The Lannets *know* people. Contacts. Okay, great, but—"

She interrupts, "Honey, they don't have a child. They got a kick out of seeing Janie in her first recital, and—"

Keith doesn't let her finish. "But they're constantly doing us favours: free theatre tickets, music camp for Janie, now this trip. The Lannets meet Hollywood execs on a producers' tour; the execs offer their place in Malibu while they're not using it, and— snap of the fingers—we're on a flight with the Lannets, straight out of a snowstorm, direct to Los Angeles."

Sometimes Meg pities Keith's suspicious nature. She says, "Maybe Art and Yolanda enjoy our company. What's wrong with that? You act as if we're not good enough to be their friends."

Keith stares at her. She can tell what he's thinking, what he's about to say. He surprises her by snugging up the towel and murmuring, "I miss Janie."

She tries to swallow, gripped by a pang of hungry mother love. "I miss her too, but I'm sure she and your mom are having a whale of a time. It's good for Janie to be independent for a week.

Don't you think it's good for us?" she says and walks over to wrap her arms around Keith.

Heat radiates from his sunburn. He winces. She loosens her arms and blows on his peeling shoulders.

"What's good about it?" he growls. "You're afraid to mess around in case the Lannets hear us from thirty-five feet away with the entire Pacific Ocean for background noise!"

She lets go of Keith. "Well, speaking of Art and Yolanda, you better get dressed. They said they wanted to talk to us about something important tonight."

"They did?" Keith empties his glass. "I knew it. The catch! They probably want us to invest in their next movie. That's what this is . . . entertaining potential investors . . . a tax write-off."

Shoving her feet into sandals, she says, "Oh, Keith! Maybe there is no catch. Maybe Art and Yolanda are just nice people." She adds, "And if they do need investment money, maybe we can find a way to help."

A few minutes later, they cross the lawn to the main house. The air is moist, sea-sweetened and salty. The sun has nearly disappeared; the palm fronds sway overhead in silhouette. Meg takes a deep breath, thinking the humid taste on her tongue is like a banquet after a life of hibernation. Her body could bulge with the surfeit of this place.

Art, dressed in linen trousers and a golf shirt, greets them at the door. "Come in, come in." He has a cordial ease, as he directs them to the front room overlooking the ocean.

Peering up from mixing a pitcher of margaritas, Yolanda coos, "Hello, you two! Oh my! Meg, you should put aloe vera on Keith's burn. Pinch some leaves from the pots on the back deck before you turn in tonight. It's soothing, with healing properties." Dressed in a sleek, aqua sundress, Yolanda crosses the room, toting two icy, margarita-filled glasses and hands them each a drink. As Keith and Meg settle into rattan chairs, Yolanda hands a glass to Art and raises her own, "Cheers," she says. "Art and I are so pleased you joined us. We were just saying we can't remember a more delightful holiday."

Meg chimes back, "We have nothing to compare it to, but this is perfect!"

Meg watches Art and Yolanda exchange looks, clink their glasses. She darts forward to sip her own drink, quickened with envy at the obvious bond between her hosts. It's different for childless couples, she thinks, no one to divert your attention from each other. Still, she can't imagine their lives without Janie.

Keith gulps his drink and smacks his lips. "This margarita is delicious."

Yolanda beams.

The first round of margaritas is accompanied by chilled shrimp salad and a watermelon soup, followed by crab quiche and crusty bread with vinaigrette.

They sit at the dining room table; outside, the foamy crests of waves are a pale glow, surging and breaking into the settled dusk.

Art makes a note about the food, waving his hand over the table like a magician, "We had this all delivered today. But, you know, Yolanda and I have decided that catering back home is just as good as LA's." He lifts his glass and salutes Keith.

By this time, Keith is on his third margarita. He smiles back. "Hey, thanks, Art. I aim to please."

Elated to see Keith enjoying himself, Meg tosses back her own drink and says, "Why not?" when Yolanda inquires if she'd like another.

"Meg! A second drink? That's not like you," Yolanda observes, "But why not, indeed? We're on vacation." Yolanda's laughter is obliterated by the grinding of ice cubes in the blender.

An hour later, the fourth pitcher of margaritas is underway. Art and Keith have lit a small fire on the beach, even though Meg is concerned it may be illegal. There is jazz music pouring out the open windows of the house. Art and Yolanda dance at the edge of the surf; the waves roll in over their bare feet, soak the bottom of Yolanda's dress and Art's rolled trousers.

Meg lies beside Keith in the still-warm sand. Raising his glass, Keith pronounces, "To our excellent friends!"

Art and Yolanda take a bow in the surf, then, laughing, they rejoin Meg and Keith by the fire. Art says, "What a fabulous night."

"This is the life," Keith agrees. "Art and Yolanda, you two have it all!"

"Well, actually, Keith," Yolanda says, starting to pile sand on her feet, "you and Meg have it all." Yolanda glances at Art and he begins to pat the sand she's been piling.

"Yes," Art agrees. "You two have Janie."

Keith grins. "Well, I won't argue there. She's our princess."

Meg nods, smiles so wide, the ocean could lap in.

Yolanda says, "That's what we wanted to talk to you about." She yanks her feet out of the sand. Loose grains scatter over the others. Art gathers her hand, holding her fingers to his lips as Yolanda begins, "I'm not able to carry a child. Art and I need a surrogate mother. We have several fertilized eggs waiting and we've chosen you, Meg."

The roar in Meg's ears obliterates the sound of surf and jazz. She stares at the blue veins in their joined hands. Then she looks for Keith as if he's gone missing. His sunburn glows like the red coals.

Art adds, "We can't imagine anyone better to carry our baby, Meg." His voice sounds faraway.

Yolanda jumps in. "For Janie, it would be like having a kind of sibling. A life-long connection."

"And of course," Art asserts, "we'll compensate you financially for the nine months, a year actually."

Meg watches Yolanda's eyes flit back and forth between the two of them. As Yolanda digs her toes back into the sand, she adds, "We don't expect an answer tonight."

Meg stands, wavers on her feet, as Keith says, "Whew, quite the honour to be asked, eh, Meg?"

Meg nods as the margaritas compete for space in her stomach. "Lots to think about," she says.

"Oh, yes," Art and Yolanda agree.

Their four heads bob like plastic dogs' on a dashboard, as Meg pulls Keith to his feet.

"Don't forget the aloe vera," Yolanda calls after them.

Back in the guest cottage, Keith says, "The saddest part is their desperation. Did you see the way Yolanda looked at you with such hope?" He pulls his t-shirt over his head before he adds, "We are indebted to them."

Ripping the aloe leaf open, Meg squashes the juice over Keith's shoulders. Her fingers still sticky, she starts cramming her belongings into a suitcase, desperate for a thinner, frozen landscape.

Ice Maker

IT'S A FRIGID NIGHT WITH A STAR-DRENCHED SKY. MY BREATH IS A fog in front of my face, misting up my glasses. If I slip my scarf off my mouth, my glasses stay clear, but my lips grow numb. Obliterated vision seems preferable to frozen lips. There's not much to see on the way to the curling rink anyway, so it doesn't matter how fogged my glasses become. A sliver of a moon offers sparse light on the shortcut path I'm taking. The winding trail of white snow is what leads me forward. The bush, rock and horizon surrounding me are black depths, but if I look up, wait for my glasses to clear, the sky emits a Milky Way Creamsicle glow. I pick out Orion's belt defining his giant girth. Sometimes, I imagine the massive proportion of his penis outlined in tiny, glittering stars. Other times, I think about being in a different place under starlight; a place, perhaps, where the stars aren't as visible, but where their meaning might be easier to comprehend. At least there's no wind tonight, which is why the stench of snowmobile exhaust hovers along the entire path—nothing to blow it clear. It lingers there long after the machines have shrieked past and the bush has swallowed their rudeness. I tug up the cedar-scented edge of my scarf and forge blindly forward.

I could be out snowmobiling. My brother Carl, his fiancée, Mona, and the rest of the gang are Saturday-night snowmobiling out to the dam. Bonfire and booze. Someone will strip naked and roll in the snow by midnight, that's my guess. And the stories they'll cart out along with their empty two-fours ... enough to tide them over until next weekend when they can rev up again. There's no fuel shortage of stories. Carl and his gang don't mind when I tag along because I never refute what they say. That's what they like best about me: they can grow a story as big as they want, right into a legend if they so desire, and I won't pull out the tape measure for exaggeration-gauging. Carl, when he's telling a whopper, holds one hand over his heart and the other palm towards the sky, and says, *As 'Becca here is my witness.* And I nod and say, *It's the truth*, and sometimes I embellish a little so that Carl can have them guzzling his story like cold beer at high noon.

I wonder what Carl would say if he knew where I was headed right now? Carl doesn't really know the Judge. The same year Carl started high school, Judge graduated from it. But Carl gets all puffed-up about him anyway, acts as if he's an expert witness when it comes to Judge. Carl used to say, *The Judge and his whole clique ... some kind of fuckin' weird.* That's probably because they read books that weren't assigned in school and went to university down east, only returning in the summers to work at the mine. That was until a few months ago, when Judge's father, Lou, the ice maker at the curling rink, had a stroke. Judge returned to Hematite then, and seems to be staying. Everybody says that Judge was called to the bar before Lou's stroke, but Carl says if he'd been called to the bar, why doesn't he open a law office in town and earn some real money defending our criminal population? *What's he doing making ice for his old man?* Carl says he's just an educated bum. Carl's fiancée, Mona, says maybe he's running away from breaking some city girl's heart ... or from knocking her up. Carl says he doubts that—*the Judge is probably a fag.*

Judge has a real name. It's Quentin. Not many people in town call him that. One exception is me ... when I'm imagining his hands roving my back and his lips nuzzling my neck, whispering legal jargon in my ear. Most people call him Judge or the Judge. Quentin doesn't seem to care what anybody calls him, but I notice that he calls everybody by their proper names.

I slide down the last ten feet of the path on my backside. When I stand, some of the snow has slipped under my parka, and my jeans are covered. I brush the snow off with my garbage mitts and stand looking at the back of the Hematite Curling Club. The parking lot is full, some cars almost run up the snow banks. The northwestern district playdowns. You can hear the rumble of the rocks from outside. Someone opens the second floor exit door to put a case of empties on the balcony and the noise from the bar wafts over me. Boisterous men's voices, and the higher pitch of female laughter. I can almost feel the happy heat descend the balcony stairs towards me. I've noticed, since I've turned legal age and am allowed upstairs, there's rarely anyone sad at the curling club bar. Lots of sad people at the hotel bars, but not at the club. Sure, you get guys pissed off about losing the big game, but they're not sad, just miffed.

I think that's what made me notice Quentin. One night when Carl, Mona, Carl's buddy and I were entered in an early, mixed bonspiel, it came down to a measure on the last rocks of our final game. Quentin had to place the stick and swing the little spring-loaded indicator round, and pronounce that our opposition's rock was closer. When he tapped it with his foot and looked at me, for a split second it seemed as if the Judge was saddened at having made this decision; as if our losing rock was the saddest thing in the world to him. A curling rink is no place for sadness. I think there's an unspoken law: if you feel sad at the club, you get yourself a drink. The next thing I saw was Quentin back upstairs nursing a Scotch. I heard they ordered a single malt into the club just for him, to keep him happy making ice. The word is that he's an even better ice maker than his old man, Lou. Sometimes, when I imagine Quentin whispering that legal jargon in my ear, his voice is so sad it splits my heart down the centre, the way a stone thrown with good weight can split a double take-out; two stones spinning in opposite directions, my heart flying out the back of the twelve-foot ring in two pieces.

I climb the exterior balcony steps and am relieved to see the shaft of light down the side of the door frame. The door is supposed to be locked, but it's often left ajar, especially when the place is crowded and busy. There's no outside handle, so I pull my garbage mitts off with my teeth, dig my fingernails into the side of the door and pull. The door opens into a corner nestled beside the bar; the closest table is the Judge's. He sits there day and evening during bonspiels, pebbling the ice between draws, or performing a measure when one's required. He's there every evening for regular club play; he's present for the afternoon business ladies' club, and for the kids' after-school round robins, just like his dad was before his stroke.

Quentin has his back to the door and the icy blast does not make him turn around, although the odd head swivels in my direction, turns back without taking notice of me there with my fogged-up glasses and my oversize parka. I wait for my glasses to clear. The place is smoky and there are dozens of conversations going on at once. I scan the room for my parents—way over in the opposite corner—before I let my eyes settle on Quentin. It's a surprise each time I witness him. His hair catches me off-guard: wavy and all one length just past his chin, parted down the middle, thick and healthy. Dad would say he should get with the times, get a haircut. Carl would say it proves he's a homo. Mom would say that kind of hair is wasted on a man. I would say nothing because it would give me away, expose me to the elements, to talk about Quentin's hair. Nothing's wasted on the Judge in my opinion.

I walk over, stand near him, and pretend to peer through the long expanse of plate glass overlooking the ice surface. All four sheets are full. I glance at the clock at the far end of the rink. Almost 10:00 p.m., last draw of the night. My eyes slide sideways and I see Quentin has a Scotch in front of him, one hand on the glass, the other arm slung over the back of his chair, relaxed into the corner of it. He turns his head to look at me, and I expect his usual dismissive glance—the one that lets me know he considers me to be slightly irritating. I unzip my jacket and pretend I need to clean my glasses on the side of my scarf. When I adjust them back on my face, Quentin is studying me as if I'm a vending machine with baffling choices, as if he's dropped in his change and I've stolen his loonie, as if he wants to shake me until something tumbles out. His fingers drum on the side of his Scotch glass, and as he turns away, his eyelids flicker as if he's seen too much. I yank off my toque and shake my hair. It's still damp from the shower and smells like apple shampoo. I turn to look directly at him. He takes a sip of Scotch, gives his attention to the eerie white of the ice sheets, the bodies sliding back and forth over them. He's ten years older than me. His face is defined by a carved timelessness: he could be graduating high school with me this spring, he could be twice my age.

Stacked on the table beside his glass is a collection of square paper drink coasters and a pencil. I have to lean closer to him to ask, "What are those for?"

He continues to stare through the plate-glass. "Mensa test," he answers. He's annoyed I've spoken.

I almost can't blurt the next question for the creeping blush ascending the sides of my cheeks: "What's Mensa?"

"A club for geniuses," he answers and looks at me then, smiles as if the two of us could never be members.

He stares at my scarf. It's my pink baby scarf which I dug out of Mom's cedar chest that morning. He says, "I like your pom-poms."

I peek at the little balls attached to the scarf ends, where they dangle between my breasts. I try to control my breathing. He glances back at my face . . . waiting, mocking, suggestive. I'd like to escape out the exit door, but I'm like a final attempt to draw to the button that stops short of the rings: I have to remain in front of the house until someone counts the score. An embarrassing bad shot. Quentin says nothing to reverse my sudden opinion that he's a prick.

"My grandma knitted this," I say to defend myself and I find the strength to turn towards the door.

He's on his feet between me and the exit. He removes the scarf from around my neck, places it on the back of his chair, then he slips my parka off my shoulders, and pulls out the chair next to him, inviting me to sit. I check the other side of the room where my parents are partying. Everybody in the place knows me. There are numerous strangers on the ice, but upstairs is packed with locals, here to watch Hematite's McMillan rink in the quarter finals. I hesitate.

"Afraid someone's going to *judge you*, Rebecca? Nothing much can happen in a place this crowded."

I continue to stand.

"Look," he says, "there are no other seats available. I can vouch for that. No one ever takes this chair. Tradition. My dad always saved a seat in case my mom could join him for the evening. After she died, no one had the nerve to ask him if they could use the chair. No one's had the nerve to ask me, either."

I think that's a good story. I continue to stand, thinking that if it's true, maybe he's not a prick. He knows I'm suspecting a bullshit factor. I can see he regrets telling me.

More to myself than to Quentin, I say, "To look at it, you might think it was just an empty chair, without its own saga."

His guffaw startles me. He shakes his head. "If anyone asks, Rebecca, just tell them there was no place else to sit."

I slide in beside him and take a desperate interest in the game below. "McMillan's down three without last rock," I observe.

"It's only the fifth end," he replies.

"Still hard being three down at this level of play."

"Anything can—and does—happen in curling," he answers me.

"Maybe curling is a metaphor for life that way," I say, still peering through the glass, trying to talk the way I imagine his sophisticated law student friends talk.

Quentin looks at me then, sips his Scotch. "Curling is just a game, Rebecca."

A roar floods the room as McMillan's opposition, the Kenora rink, misses its last rock of the end, leaving McMillan with three points to tie. Everyone talks at once: *Wide of his broom. Misread the ice. Might have had it with less weight. He shouldn't have been playing the double. That's gotta hurt. Even with less ice, that was a bad angle to attempt. Should have played the come-around draw. The four-foot was open. Lucky break for McMillan.* One shot; countless versions of what went wrong. Those who aren't sitting by the glass jostle forward from their tables to take a look. People from the window seats head straight to the bar to refill their drinks before the start of the next end. The other games are being ignored. Then there's a call for a measure on sheet one.

"They need the Judge down there," someone from the far end of the room calls.

Quentin rises from his chair. "Do you want anything?" he pauses to ask me before he heads down to measure the rocks.

I stare up at him. What do I want? Every scrap of his knowledge, every molecule of his body, every story he knows and has never thought to tell. But more than that, I want to know if it's possible that he could want the same from me.

"From the bar, Rebecca? Anything from the bar?"

I shake my head no.

He goes down to the ice surface. I watch him measure two stones, pointing—without hesitation—to the one closest to the button. I close my eyes and think how simple some decisions can be. When I open them, Quentin is placing a glass of Scotch in front of me.

"Don't worry if you don't like it. It won't go to waste."

I swirl the contents of the glass. The ice cubes chase each other around. A single sip burns its way down my throat. I try not to wince. I say, "Who knew spoonable medicine could become an acquired taste?"

Quentin does not respond to my joke. He reaches for my scarf, lays it across his lap, fingers the pom-poms, drops it on the table, abruptly stands. He says something to Ernie behind the bar, to which Ernie nods and waves his hand as if there's no problem.

Quentin returns to the table, picks up my parka and asks me if I'd like to take a walk. I shrug and stand. My lungs have forgotten the simple task of breathing. Quentin puts on his own jacket, drapes my scarf around my neck, holds onto the pom-pom ends for a moment before he lets go. Tucking the square coasters and pencil into his jacket pocket, he steers me out the balcony exit.

There's a part of me expecting to hear my father's voice behind us calling me back, but we're past the spread of parking lot light and down the street into relative darkness and no one seems to care.

Quentin asks, "You don't mind missing the end of the game?"

It's the last thing on my mind, but it's hard to know what to say now that we're alone. "Curling is just a game, Quentin."

"Touché," he says. His word hangs visibly in the air for a brief moment and disappears into the next breath. We walk in silence, until we arrive within a block of the hospital.

He says, "I hope you don't mind, I'm going to pop in and say good-night to my dad, Lou."

I mind a lot, but I don't say. At least it explains what we're doing out here in the friggin' cold.

Quentin rings a night bell and a moment later, a nurse appears and unlocks the door for the extended care wing.

"Quentin," she says and smiles. She's about Quentin's age, and apart from using his real name, I notice she purses her lips when she speaks, "We didn't expect you tonight."

"It's not too late?" Quentin asks.

"No. He's awake. I just gave him his meds."

I mumble as I try to wipe the fog from my glasses, "I'll wait here."

"Hey," Quentin says, "I was hoping you'd come in, say hi, and help me with something."

"Help you?" I ask. I'm no nurse, that much I know about myself.

"The Mensa thing, remember?"

"The genius club?" I say and I'm confused.

"Just bear with me," he pleads.

I follow him down a corridor of dim lights and antiseptic smell. There's liniment mixed in to boot. I want to turn tail and make a break for it, but Quentin takes my hand as we enter a small corner room.

"Hey, Dad!" Quentin says.

I barely recognize Lou, the ice maker, lying there, half-propped in the bed. His mouth droops on one side, while the other half contorts to say something that's not comprehensible.

"Dad, this is Rebecca."

"Hi, Mr. Wiltson," I say, my voice creaking.

"Dad, don't worry. You look great. Extra grooming tonight from the nurses? Must have known you were expecting company."

The strain around Lou's eyes evaporates. I sense if he could smile, he would be beaming at his son.

"Pretty exciting day," Quentin continues. "I have all the results here except for the last game. We left after the fifth end. McMillan's in a tie game. But we wanted to bring you up-to-date, tonight." He pulls the square drink coasters from his pocket and hands them to me. I hold onto them, thankful for something to concentrate on other than poor Lou Wiltson.

"Okay, I'm doing these from memory," Quentin says to his dad. "Rebecca is going to make sure I don't screw up or cheat. Ready, Rebecca?" he asks me. I look at the coasters and see each one of them has a game result written on the back.

Quentin begins, "Okay, the 9:00 a.m. draw, we had Sutherland over Petrosko, 8 to 7. Came down to last rocks there. Sutherland had to draw to the four-foot to win. Sheet two had Carrington over Smith, a wipe-out, 8 to 2, after nine ends. Sheet three, McMillan over the Fort Frances rink, that young foursome, with Bellamo skipping, another close shave, 6 to 5. Bellamo had the point to tie and McMillan had to make his last shot to avoid the extra end. He had to squeak past his own guard to knock Bellamo's rock out. He lost his shooter, so it was a good thing he was one up coming home. How am I doing?" Quentin asks me.

There are no details on the coasters, just the final scores, so I can't determine the accuracy of his play-by-play tidbits. Lou is eating it up, though, so I reason it doesn't matter if the details are true or not. I give Quentin the thumbs up and he continues until he's gone through the entire day's draws without a mistake. Then he says to Lou, "But I figure McMillan's going down tonight. Carrington out of Kenora hasn't lost a game yet. We won't know until the morning. Care to lay a little wager?"

One side of Lou's mouth twists and he grunts. Quentin pulls a loonie from his pocket, shows Lou. Then he opens Lou's top bedside drawer and takes a loonie from his dad's wallet. "A buck each! I'll leave it here under the African violet for safe-keeping. I'll be by tomorrow morning to collect!"

Even through the haze of meds and damage, Lou's eyes utter love.

Quentin smiles at him, "Ah, you think you've got me, eh, Dad? Well, remember what you always said; I taught Rebecca your motto tonight, right, Rebecca?

I smile at Quentin, and say to Lou, "Anything can—and does—happen in curling."

Lou manages to lift his right hand as if I've said something smart.

Before Quentin bends over to kiss his dad's forehead, he pushes his own hair back behind his ears. "We'll see who's right tomorrow. Get some sleep. I have to take Rebecca home now. 'Night."

Back out in the cold air, I hand Quentin the paper coasters. He returns them to his pocket. "Thanks," he says. "When I was a kid, Dad got a kick out of the way I memorized things. He said I could learn anything, even how to make ice—used to let me tag along with him every weekend."

Sadness again.

My brother Carl's voice barges into my thoughts. I imagine him pronouncing judgement on what just transpired: *Weirdest fuckin' story I ever heard, 'Becca. Must be your glasses or something attracting the weirdoes!*

I say to Quentin, "It must be a comfort for Lou to have you home right now."

We are back in the parking lot of the curling club before Quentin says, "Yeah, I feel guilty about half-lying to him."

I laugh, incredulous. "I knew you were embellishing those game details!"

"No, not that," he says as he unlocks the passenger door of Lou's old truck and holds it open for me, before he adds, "I half-lied about taking you home."

The tires are frozen cubes of ice. I have to scrape the inside of the windshield as we drive, the heater's not working right. The condensation curls off the window in short frosty bursts. The rasping sound makes the back of my teeth ache. We thump into Quentin's driveway. Peeling the mat away from the doorstep, he takes a key from under it. It won't work in the lock until he holds it between his hands and breathes on it for a moment. Waiting there, I'm certain I will shiver myself apart into frozen shards.

He doesn't stop to turn on any lights. He undresses me in the pitch dark of the kitchen. His cold fingers and the green numbers on the microwave clock are my anchors, as the furnace hum spreads through me. I am hungry for the sight of Quentin's wavy hair and the trace of his naked skin. He carries me upstairs and when I protest at his removing my glasses, he whispers my objections are overruled.

Lying beside Quentin, the curtains thrown open to the creamy glow of starlight, I think I've found a place where truth is possible. But finding truth and telling it are two different stories. Some tales, like the ones about the night you lose your virginity, are yours and yours alone . . . as unreadable as a sheet of badly made ice.

The Gift

AFTER HER DIVORCE, JOY CHOSE NOT TO SEE OTHER MEN. SHE
had Pina and Sasha to think about. Daughters. Five and three
years old. She reapplied at the school where she'd taught before
her children's birth, a small elementary school populated by
women, right down to the principal and day custodian. Pina and
Sasha's father moved back to the States. He sent cheques in the
mail for the girls. Joy never saw him again. She didn't miss her ex
or the company of men in general. The girls filled her life. She
loved the way they tumbled into the car, full of chatter, to go to
the mall or out for an ice cream; the smell of their hair after a
bath; the way Pina tried so hard to please her by completing her
homework right after school; Sasha's robot impersonations; the
fact they turned to her with all their hurts and triumphs, from a
classmate's jealous word to landing the lead in the Christmas pag-
eant; the snuggling way they bounced into her bed Saturday
mornings and the three of them nested there, reading the funnies
and working on the crossword.

By the time Pina turned eleven and Sasha nine, Joy's mother,

Fernie, suggested that perhaps it was time for Joy to start going out on her own a bit. Fernie said, *I'll babysit so you can go to a grown-up movie, or for dinner with a friend … a man perhaps. You're still young, Joy, but youth fades; you look in the mirror one day and it's too late.* Joy became angry and didn't call her mother for almost a month.

She did call her sister, Isabelle, who after witnessing Joy's divorce had quit her job as a facilitator for a utilities company and opened a dating service. Isabelle, with six years' savvy in the business, chose her words as if they were filed on rotary flip cards, *It's natural for Mom to worry about you, but if you're not open to a relationship, success is unlikely. Don't sweat it, Joy.* And then while she avoided suggesting that Joy use her service, she made a point of chatting about the success stories; the love-at-first-sights, the kismet, the fairy-tale weddings. She told Joy that she had just stocked one of her closets with boxed stacks of fine, crystal champagne glasses—gifts for her clients' nuptials. This, Isabelle said, would save her a lot of time shopping, plus, since it was a tax write-off, there was only one receipt to keep track of each year. Love is lucrative, Isabelle had told Joy.

The year Pina turned twelve, and Sasha turned ten, Joy was the first to find out that Isabelle planned to expand her dating service onto the Internet. Isabelle left a card with the website address beside Joy's home computer. On the back of the card, she jotted down a password that would allow Joy to browse without being billed. Joy ignored the card, shoved it in the back of a desk drawer, until the evening when she was tucking in Pina and Sasha, and the younger blurted out, "Mommy, Pina's got a boyfriend at school!"

"I do not," Pina squealed. "I hate boys." Little red blotches appeared on her cheeks.

Sasha's soft blue eyes grew big and indignant. "Then why were you holding hands with *Jake the Snake* outside at recess?"

"*Jake the Snake?!*" Joy exclaimed.

Sasha nodded. "That's what everybody calls him, 'cause he kind of hisses when he talks."

"You're a liar!" Pina roared, and hurled her stuffed monkey across the room towards Sasha's bed.

Stunned by Pina's vehemence, Joy retrieved the monkey before the situation could escalate, and settled it on Pina's pillow. She brushed Pina's hair out of her eyes and rubbed her back.

"Leave your sister alone, Sasha," Joy implored. "Stop teasing and go to bed now."

Joy turned out their light. A dark curtain drew around her. *Did Pina hate men? Would she choose a mate unwisely? Jake the Snake sounded hideous—a beady-eyed boy with a flicking tongue. Had Joy failed to provide a positive male role model for her daughters?* She switched on her computer, typed the password Isabelle had given her and spent several hours clicking through files.

Isabelle would not arrange Joy's date with Baron—wouldn't even create her profile for him to consider—until she took Joy for a haircut, highlights, eyebrow plucking, and a few new wardrobe items, including a set of matching undergarments. She then advised Joy that it wasn't a good idea to choose a potential date on looks alone, that she might want to rethink Baron, that he might be out of her league, that a man who spent a disproportionate amount of time outside the country travelling for business, and who then dedicated his leisure time to re-establishing falcons in both their natural and urban habitats might not be an ideal match for her. *You know,* she said to Joy, *I've been around long enough to know that no one can predict what will happen in matters of the heart, but you're my sister, and I'm trying to give you the best advice I can from my experience.* Joy wasn't open to Isabelle's professional counselling.

Joy met Baron for their first date at a Chinese restaurant of his choice. At first touch of his cordial handshake, something inside her sat up and brushed itself off. An hour later she caught herself remembering she had children. Their sweet faces flashed in her head; but immersed in the glow of the red lantern at their table,

Joy found it easy to relax and give herself back to the present moment ... to listen and think of nothing other than Baron's explanation of how he'd become interested in raptors. She began to memorize his features. He wasn't drop-dead gorgeous, but he was well proportioned: nose not too large, lips not too thin, hair not too long. By dessert and liqueur—after she noticed the faint, crinkly laugh lines around his eyes as he chuckled at the story of her childhood budgie bird's penchant for beer—she began lusting for her own beak and talons, something to sharpen on Baron's skin.

After a month of seeing him, Joy arranged a date at the zoo so he could meet her daughters. Sasha said he was nice and had a nice SUV. Pina said his cologne made her feel sick. On the next date, Baron wore unscented deodorant and drove them into the mountains for a gourmet picnic lunch. A short off-road trail led them to a spectacular view of a river gorge with steep cliff walls. They ate in a meadow and then hiked along the gorge ledge. Sasha exclaimed that she loved seeing the peregrine falcon nest through Baron's binoculars. Pina muttered that her feet hurt and that Baron had expensive hiking boots that made it easy to walk around on the jagged rocks all day.

On the following Saturday morning, Baron took Joy and the girls to his office tower and showed them the young falcons that had hatched in the nesting box outside his window the previous month. He had a photo of them when they were awkward, odd-looking, white fluff-ball babies with beaks, and he explained that now they were almost full-grown and ready to start flying and hunting. *If we're lucky*, he said, *we'll see the parents fly by with prey and the young falcons will try to snatch it from the parents' talons. That's how they teach their offspring to hunt for themselves.*

Sasha said the young falcons were handsome and asked if she could bring her classmates to see them. Pina said the black streaks under the birds' eyes made them look like camouflaged soldiers; she referred to them as a family of savage killers who preyed on harmless pigeons. When Baron tried to explain that pigeons made up a small portion of the urban falcons' diet, Pina sat in his leather office chair and spun in circles. Joy frowned at Pina; what needed to be said to her daughter would embarrass all of them. Pina tilted her head back and continued spinning. Joy slid a hopeless look of apology in Baron's direction. He shrugged and smiled at her, shook his head to let her know that Pina's actions didn't bother him. His willingness to overlook her child's rude behaviour was like a flute of champagne for Joy's thirsting heart. She fizzed and bubbled with gratitude.

That evening, Joy left the girls overnight with her mother, Fernie, and she didn't return home until morning.

Baron departed for Hong Kong on business the next week. Joy doubted he would fulfil his promise to call when he returned. She wept, sometimes with relief, sometimes with despair. Wasn't the idea of dating again to help Pina? Why did Pina's behaviour frustrate her?

Isabelle dropped over and suggested that Joy not take things to heart; maybe peek at prospects #22 and #35 in the data base. Fernie reminded Joy that in a few short years neither of her daughters would be caring one bit about what she was doing, and that Joy should forge ahead at rebuilding a life for herself. Sasha said she wished that the school year wasn't ending because now she couldn't bring her classmates to see the birds. Pina bought Joy a jumbo-size Swiss chocolate bar with her own money on the last day of school.

On the first Saturday of summer break, Joy ignored the girls as they clambered into her bed for the crossword and funnies snuggle. She locked herself in the bathroom. In the tub, with the cordless phone on the floor beside her, she read fashion magazine make-up tips. When the girls knocked on the door to protest, Joy called back, *It's the first week of vacation. Aren't I entitled to relax?*

Baron kept his promise to call upon his return from Hong Kong. Joy stopped taking extended magazine baths. Isabelle insisted Joy go to a tanning booth before she saw Baron again.

He took her to the same Chinese restaurant as on their first date and confessed he'd missed her. She blushed through her faint tan; it went unnoticed under the red lantern glow. Baron told her he'd found a small gift in Kowloon, and from his blazer pocket he removed a box, which he placed on the table and slid towards her with his fingertips. She opened it. Strung on a gold chain was a blue-green opal with a fiery-red streak down one side.

Joy bit her lip as she strung it around her neck. "I can't believe you bought me something so precious . . . all the way from Hong Kong!"

He didn't respond at first. He glanced at the opal, then at her face, before he nodded and said, "You know, while I was trying to pick the precise gem for you, I finally understood why male peregrines fly those complex courtship flights: we males have such a desperate need to impress."

"I love it," she said. "It couldn't be more perfect."

Later, he gave the girls each a little silk wallet with a Chinese coin inside, a red one for Pina, a blue one for Sasha. Sasha threw herself at Baron and hugged him. Pina said, *Thank-you.* Joy smiled with relief. Then Pina told Baron that she'd read in a book at school that some people thought opals were bad luck.

A week later Baron called to say that his parents were travelling to the city for the weekend and that he'd like to have Joy meet them for dinner. He asked Joy if she'd mind wearing her necklace, as his father was an amateur lapidary and would enjoy seeing the stone.

The afternoon of the date, Isabelle arrived, air-conditioner blasting against a scorching summer heat. She collected Joy, dropped off the girls at Fernie's for the night, and took Joy shopping for a sleeveless black dress with the perfect neckline to set off an opal. The day wore on into a hot, humid late afternoon. Isabelle advised Joy not to dress until the last minute. *You'll wilt otherwise,* Isabelle cautioned. *Keep the linen crisp until he arrives.* Joy found the heat made her too languorous to rush anyway. She sat in the shade and watched the sky blister with thunderheads before she went inside to shower under a coolish spray. Just before he was scheduled to arrive, Joy slipped into the black dress and crossed to her jewellery box. The necklace wasn't where she remembered putting it. Puzzled, she emptied the box twice before broadening her search ... the dresser, the closet, the bathroom. The doorbell rang. As she met his greeting kiss, she confessed that she had temporarily misplaced the necklace.

"You lost the opal?" Baron said and shoved his hands into his trouser pockets, jingled loose change.

"No! Not lost. It's in the house, I know it is," Joy assured him. "I could continue looking right now, but we'll keep your parents waiting and we'll be late for the reservations."

Baron's parents, Evelyn and Herb, both tanned and fit-looking in the back seat said, "Don't worry. We'll see it next time."

Glancing at Baron, Joy said, "I feel terrible about misplacing it."

"It's just an object, Joy," Evelyn said with a wide, gracious smile. "The important thing is we're able to meet you this evening."

Baron's father said, "Evelyn here lost her engagement ring the first year we were married."

"And Herb's never let me forget it," Baron's mother quipped. "He finally replaced it for our twenty-fifth anniversary."

Baron added, "Dad cut the raw diamond himself."

"Remarkable," Joy declared as Evelyn stuck out her ring finger and the diamond sparkled in the dim interior light.

"Yes," Baron muttered, "one of the reasons I hoped Dad could take a look at the opal." He stepped hard on the brake at the next stop light and then stomped on the accelerator. As the evening progressed Baron's mood did not improve. Joy tried to focus on his parents' anecdotes and cheerful banter. She smiled at Baron's askance glances. Perhaps he'd heard his parents' stories too many times before; perhaps he wasn't thinking of the misplaced opal at all.

On the way home, a driving rain beat against the windshield. When Baron stopped the SUV in Joy's driveway, he said, *You'd better make a run for it.* She dashed through the downpour and stood just inside her door, her black dress plastered to her body, her hair dripping wet on her bare shoulders. Baron's headlights flashed once in her eyes as he backed down the driveway and then swung an arc of light across the empty street. He hadn't seen her to the door; no mention of calling again. She watched the unforgiving red glow of his tail-lights until they disappeared from view.

Not bothering to remove her wet dress, she began to search the house for the opal. She went from room to room shuffling papers, checking under cushions, picking up stray items of clothing, checking the laundry hamper, shaking out the pile of magazines from the bathroom. Every new, unturned, possibility had her imagining her telephone call to Baron in the morning ... *tucked in my lingerie drawer the whole time.* She went to sleep that night and dreamed she found it. When she awoke to the realization it was still missing, she buried her head in the pillow and thumped the mattress.

Later, after collecting the girls at Fernie's, she explained what had happened, asking for their assistance in the search. Both girls nodded. Sasha asked Joy if she'd checked under the sofa and chairs, and she crawled around the living room, every once in awhile acting as if she might have found it. After a few moments, Sasha suggested that Joy look in her jewellery box again.

"Maybe 'cause you were in a hurry, you just missed it," Sasha said.

"No, Sasha, sweetie, it's definitely not there."

"But you should check anyway."

"It's not there."

"Pleee-ase, just check," she pleaded.

Joy opened the box and checked each slot and the three little drawers as well, while Sasha stood at the door craning her neck to see.

"Like I said, Sasha, it's not here."

Sasha stared at her mother, then ran down the hall to her bedroom.

Joy followed her.

Sasha, frantic, whispered, "You said you'd put it back, Pina!"

"What?" Joy flew into the room. "Did you take my necklace, Pina?"

"No!" Pina exclaimed.

"Yes, she did," Sasha shouted.

"I did not. Sasha's lying again, Mom!"

Joy felt a sudden surge of heat inside her chest. She looked from one girl to the other.

"No, I'm not lying," Sasha said, pouting. "Pina made me promise I wouldn't tell when I found it in her backpack last night at Grandma's."

Joy closed her eyes and tried to breathe calmly. "Pina, why would you take my necklace?"

"I didn't!"

Joy grabbed Pina's backpack off the floor and flung out her pyjamas, dirty socks and underwear, her hairbrush, a paperback book, her stuffed monkey. She checked the outside pockets; nothing there but a nickel and a pair of mismatched hair barrettes.

Joy insisted, "Pina, I want you to give the necklace back to me!"

Pina flew for the door, but Joy grabbed her by the shoulders and shook her. "Where is it?" she demanded.

Sasha wailed, "Just give it to her, Pina!"

"Yes! Give it to me!" Joy shrieked.

Tears burst out of Pina's eyes, but her lips stayed clamped shut. Joy pushed her out of the way. She ripped the blankets off Pina's bed. Finding nothing, she wrenched out dresser drawers and dumped them on the floor.

"Where is it you little, lying thief?" Joy screeched.

Sasha grabbed Pina, hugged her, sobbed, "Please, Pina, give it back to Mommy!"

Joy tore open the girls' closet and whipped out hangers and dresses, jackets and shoes. She hovered over Pina's desk, snatched books from the shelf, emptied crayons, markers and papers onto the floor.

Pina and Sasha tried to flee the room. Joy whirled and lunged at Pina, grasping hold of a hank of her hair, forcing her to twist around. That was when Joy noticed the little red Chinese wallet clutched in Pina's hand. Joy wrenched it from her fingers, and at the same moment Pina tore free of Joy's grip. The two girls fled down the hall. They huddled together, perched behind the locked bathroom door. Joy yanked open the wallet, dug under the Chinese coin. As she drew out the necklace, she saw the gold setting was bent, mangled. She turned it over. A blue-green piece of the opal fell to the floor. The other half, the jagged-edged, fiery-red streak, remained clutched in Joy's trembling fingers.

Caution: Mother Playing

CAROLE WAKES UP AND STANDS WITH HER ELBOWS RESTING ON the window sill, thinking back to a time when a morning blanketed by a heavy snowfall would be something wondrous to her. When she was her twin sons' age, she would draw back her bedroom curtains to the unexpected insulated hush of a whitened world, and she would feel as if she were plugged into a trickle charger, a humming tingle coursing through her. She loved the trickery of snow, the way it transformed a landscape, encouraging her to believe her own future could be something extraordinary. If the world could reinvent itself overnight, why couldn't she?

Slick roads. Fender benders. Ditch roll-overs. This morning Carole tries to ignore these thoughts. The twins will be getting their beginner permits in a few months. She clamps her teeth to keep from expressing her concerns out loud; she doesn't want the boys to become nervous drivers before they sit behind a steering wheel. She strives to be the kind of mother who instills confidence and self-esteem, who encourages her children to dream possibilities. Too often, she catches herself cautioning them, unable to stop, as if the warnings themselves, issued often and with zeal, will somehow be enough to protect them.

She forces a smile as she packs their lunches, says, "I'm looking forward to this afternoon's performance!"

"What time are you arriving at school to pick up the instruments, Mom?" This is Ross, the organizer.

"Mom, have you seen my music folder?" This is Robbie, the disorganized.

"It's on your desk, Robbie," she answers. "I'll try and arrive a few minutes early because traffic will be slow today . . . with the snow." She nods at her self-restraint. The boys are already out the door, tossing "Whoa, snow's as high as my knees and it's still coming down," and "See ya later"s over their shoulders.

"Play your best! Break a leg!" she calls after them. She doesn't know if saying "Good luck" bestows bad luck on musicians as well as actors, but she doesn't want to take any chances.

Carole stacks the breakfast dishes in the dishwasher and switches it on. She wipes the counters, and adds *peanut butter* to the magnetized grocery list on the fridge. She hops in the shower, shampoos and body washes, dries her hair, directs hair spray right to the roots to attain a little height in her style, brushes and flosses her teeth. She dresses in jeans and her best sweater: she doesn't want to embarrass the boys by looking like the stay-at-home mom, but little else in her wardrobe compares with what the working mothers wear whenever they find the time to attend. She pours fresh water for Tiptoe, the poodle. She throws a load of towels in the wash machine, and calls the orthodontist's office to see if Robbie's replacement retainer is ready—she may be able to swing by there on the way home and save herself a second trip into the city. She crosses off the orthodontist call from her to-do list and adds *call Wendy re: Stitch Club potluck*. She dials Finley's number and leaves a message on his voice mail, reminding him that if he can take a late lunch, he can catch the boys' performance at the concert hall, 1:30 sharp. She looks for and finds her purse, checks for her van keys. She calls her mother and suggests to her that, considering the dreadful weather, maybe she not venture out to the concert today after all. Her mother wants to hear the whole story again of how the boys' school band won the Junior Competition the previous spring and was awarded a workshop and performance with the city's renowned symphony conductor, Klaus Loostroff. Checking her watch, Carole tells her mother she has to go.

Before she starts the van, she pauses to check her image in the sun visor mirror. She takes note of nothing there, as if she's looked, but hasn't bothered to see herself. For a brief moment, she feels, as she often does, that she's forgotten something. What could it be that wants to be tied around her finger like string? What could be worth remembering? She drives carefully to the school—her windshield wipers thwacking at winter, her tires struggling to get a grip.

Anxious energized teenagers in their unzipped parkas, white shirts, hunter green cummerbunds and matching bow ties, begin to fill the back of Carole's emptied van with tubas, French horns, cymbals, baritone saxes and a gong. The band director, Madame L'Heurtemps, clucks and hums a single note when she sees they are running out of space. Her other volunteer driver has not shown up, on this, Madame L'Heurtemps' most important day of her musical teaching career. She wraps and unwraps her scarf; there is no room on the school bus for the instruments. She directs her students, "Take the tubas out of their cases and put them on Mrs. Gander's passenger seats. *Ici. Ici. Maintenant*, roll the gong up there right between the seats, and the cymbals … on top, on top! *Bien! Voilà!*" She swipes her hands together and beams at Carole when it all fits in. It seems a bit precarious to Carole, but she doesn't want to argue with Madame L'Heurtemps, who commented recently, "Neither you nor your husband have any musical inclination, yet the twins have much talent. *Très étrange, n'est-ce pas?* Excellent instruction goes a long way."

Carole craves praise of her children. The *much talent* rings in her ears as she checks that the van door is clear of instruments and shuts it. She looks up and sees the twins waving to her from inside the school bus. She brushes the snow out of her hair and returns their waves before she settles back in behind the wheel.

Hours later, after the concert, the winter conditions are worse. The snowplows are not keeping pace with accumulations; intersections resemble unshovelled skating rinks. The wind has increased. Visibility is down. Carole, however, hums to herself as she inches along with the afternoon traffic. She was so moved by the music that it continues to ride along inside her. How ironic, she is thinking, that the last piece they performed was called "Into the Storm."

It takes close to an hour for the emergency crew, utilizing the Jaws of Life, to extricate Carole from the mangled metal of van and musical instruments. Consciousness drifts in and out. She hears sirens and Madame L'Heurtemps wailing *Mon Dieu! Mon Dieu!* She sees Klaus Loostroff's white baton coaxing the band to crescendo. She is on her feet applauding. She hears Robbie, desperate, *Hang on, Mom.* She cannot hear Ross; he is playing his French horn on the concert hall stage, but there is no sound. She hears the shrieking screech of rotating blade teeth slicing through metal; the hiss and spit of a compressor. She smells the white heat of sparks. There are so many strangers repeating her name, *Carole, try not to move. Carole? Carole. Carole? Carole.* Why does her body feel like a purple-green bruise—a grape skin split—too ripe to touch? Why can't she see? Why does she awaken—not remembering the falling asleep? What is that other peculiar hum vibrating inside her? Are those snowflakes melting on her face? She does not remember the transport truck skidding into her van; she is unaware of the ambulance ride. Did she forget something? In the sun visor mirror, she sees her twin babies in their car seats on a busy boulevard. She left them sitting atop the trunk of her old blue car when she drove away. They tumbled onto the boulevard. There is no place for her to turn around in the heavy traffic. She is driving away from her babies in the wrong direction, while someone plays the trumpet. If only she could turn around! She must turn around!

The first time she wakes, Carole thinks she's just had her tonsils out . . . the strange feeling in her throat and the soft touch of the hospital flannel sheet on top of her. She has not slept under flannel since she was five. But there's a difference. Her head. Is it clamped in a too-small hat? The room is dim and when she reaches up, her arm drags its own weight and IV tubes along with it. She touches her hair, which has not been washed in a week. Some of it is missing. A monitor beeps, a nurse flies in from around the corner and stands over her, placing her hands on Carole's shoulders, making eye contact.

"Mrs. Gander. Carole? It's okay. You're okay. You're in the hospital. Your family will be so happy that you've woken. They've gone home to rest. I'm going to call Dr. Webb. Do you understand what I'm saying to you?"

Carole nods her head.

"Good." The nurse nods with her. "Good, Carole."

"Are you in pain?"

Carole nods again, not knowing the answer.

"I'm going to add a painkiller to your drip. You'll feel better right away."

The next time she wakes, she smells antiseptic and steamed breakfast, and she sees Finley. He stands with his back to her; here and there the white of his scalp shines exposed through his thinning hair. She remembers he was out of shampoo. She was supposed to buy some. She can't remember if it was on her list, or if it was, its brand name. Finley is listening to the doctor who speaks in a low, rapid voice, not inviting interruption.

"As we've discussed, there are no other major physical impediments: no broken bones, no internal bleeding. Contusions, abrasions and cuts, of course. But miraculous, really! It's the head injury which is puzzling. The concussion she suffered was minor, not in keeping with a six-day coma. Peculiar, really. I'm conferring with colleagues in California. We're monitoring it. Good sign she's regaining consciousness, of course.

That's the focus. She's sedated, but we'll be easing her out of that and we'll see."

Carole feels sorry for Finley. He likes to have all the answers—no wait and sees. She is surprised she knows this when there are other questions crowding in.

The men turn toward her and Finley takes a stride before crumpling at the side of her bed. "You're awake again. Thank God." He clasps her hand and kisses her palm, avoiding the IV line. "How are you feeling?"

She wants to ask, "Where are the boys?" But when she tries to form the words, her throat constricts and her tongue feels like an inflated balloon, too large and pressurized to do anything but bob and float in her mouth.

"There's no rush, Mrs. Gander. Take it easy. I'm Doctor Webb. You've been in a car accident, but you're doing very well, really." He steps closer to the bed. "Would you just look at the light for me?" He waves a tiny pen-light, shines it in her eyes, moves it behind his back, shines it in her eyes and pronounces, "Very good."

After two days of her not being able to speak, Ross brings his mother a pad of note paper from home and her favourite pen. Robbie sits on the bed beside her and says, "So what do you remember, Mom? Do you want to talk about it? Don't write *Did you do your homework?* We did that, right, Ross?"

Ross doesn't answer his twin. He watches his mother draw two sets of five parallel lines. She tries to write down how much she loves them; how she thinks they may have grown in the week she was in the coma, but she fills in the lines with squiggles.

Ross winces. "But you know where you are, right, Mom?"

She nods.

Ross adds, "And I'm Robbie, right?"

She raises an eyebrow at him and shakes her head no.

"We could never fool you!" Robbie blurts.

They all smile. Then they look down at the piece of paper again and their smiles fade.

Robbie says, "Don't worry, Mom. Dr. Webb says when you come home, you'll improve. Nice back-to-normal home environment." Ross and Robbie nod in unison.

When Carole walks into her home, she has an initial feeling of not having lived there for a very long time. She notices the kitchen counters are clean. She is thankful for this. Such a kindness, she thinks, clean counters that you, yourself, haven't wiped. She thinks she should check to see if the towels she put in the wash before the accident are still sitting in the machine, stale and musty; but instead she turns on the radio and sits at the kitchen table looking out the window at the snow-tipped evergreens; glancing from time to time at her husband and sons bustling around the stove fixing her lunch; patting Tiptoe on the head whenever he comes to sniff her.

The next morning, through vigorous shaking of her head, she communicates to them that she doesn't want them staying home from work or school to take care of her.

"You're certain you'll be alright?" Finley confirms several times. He adds, "I'll call you every couple of hours." When he realizes the implications of what he's said, he knuckles his hand over his mouth. When he speaks again, he keeps his clenched hand on his lips, "You ... you could ... hmmm ... you could tap three times on the receiver if you want me to come home. Like an SOS."

Her anger flares at him. Her breath rasps and although she knows it's not Finley's fault that she can't speak or write down words on a piece of paper, she wants to throw things at him, pound her fists into the soft flesh of his back where it sits above his belt, even while she's thankful for him. She doesn't want the scheduled appointments for MRI scans and EEG's; she just wants to be better. She puts her head into her arms on the kitchen table, and Finley brushes the back of her neck with his lips.

"I'll stay home," he murmurs as the boys back out of the room and gather their books at the door. Her head swivels up and she shakes it vehemently again. Finley adds, "I'll call your mother. She offered to stay with you all day. Or, Wendy and the girls from Stitch Club said they could take turns checking on you."

This time Carole shakes her head until little black spots jump in her vision. She is determined to be alone and cure herself this very day. She stands, hands Finley his coat, kisses him and smiles. She'll be all right, she is trying to say. He shrugs his acquiescence.

The house is muted, emitting only the cyclical forced air hum of the furnace and the clicking of Tiptoe's nails as he follows Carole around the uncarpeted rooms. She turns into the master bedroom, sits on the rumpled bed and takes a long look at herself in the dresser mirror. The bruise on the right side of her face, where the tuba banged into her, is fading. The cut on her forehead is healing—the stitches the last thing to come out before she left the hospital. The dark circles under her eyes are still puffy, but improved.

Tiptoe jumps into her lap and licks her chin. She laughs and her throat croaks out its first audible sound since the accident. Both she and the poodle are caught off guard. Tiptoe shuffles from one foot to the other, kneading Carole's leg, as if to regain his balance. Carole takes a deep breath and tries to say, "Good boy, Tippy." From her mouth issues the sound of a few ragged flute notes, the kind played with bad *embouchure*, the lips incorrectly held. Tiptoe leaps off her lap, then looks at her before he scurries under the bed. "It's all right, boy. Come here, Tiptoe," is what she tries to say; this time the notes float out more solid and sweet, but flute, nonetheless. Carole crouches on her knees beside the bed and rocks there for a moment. Trying again, desperate for word sounds, she lowers her chin and concentrates, taps the floor in front of her. "Tippy, come here, boy. It's all right. It's all right." Clarinet emerges instead. She can't sustain the mellow warbling very well. The notes grate down her spine. Horrified, listening to Tiptoe whine under the bed, she tries again. She manages to hold the notes steadier with more resonance, but at the same time she feels a scream rising in her throat. It comes out the screeching *blat* of an alto saxophone on a misfingered, overblown A sharp.

She clutches her throat, then crunches a pillow around her ears. What the hell is the matter with her? She gulps air, terrified to make another sound. She crawls under the duvet until her heart stops pounding and she wishes she could summon just one day of her life before the accident . . . either that, or the sweet relief of sleep. Neither comes to her. She stares instead at the ceiling; remembers cleaning out the tiny black insects from the glass light fixture over her bed sometime before the accident, crossing it off her list of things to do. Oh, what you can accomplish in a day when you aren't scrambling about, searching for your voice.

From the bedside table, she removes a sheet of stationery and a pen and attempts to write down what has happened. The two sets of five parallel lines appear and then the squiggles take on a definite shape of quarter and half-notes. A treble clef emerges. Its appearance in the centre of a line disturbs her. It doesn't belong there; this much, she knows. The piece of paper is covered in a random array of musical notes before she slumps back into the pillows. What has happened to her? People who bump their heads on concrete don't become sidewalks; people who graze their skulls while fainting in the bathroom don't become porcelain sinks; yet her tuba conk has turned her into a musical whacko. Maybe it's the painkillers—but she's down to just one at bedtime . . .

The week following her discovery, Carole strains each day to make a human voice sound come out of her throat. By the beginning of the second week, she decides that perhaps the abnormality requires something extraordinary to affect it. She becomes determined to find the means: she stands on her head and speaks; holds her hand under scalding hot tap water; she blindfolds and earmuffs herself to cut off outside stimuli, then meditates. Through the ear muffs, she hears a sitar. She finally gets behind the wheel of the new van and drives the highway at fifty kilometres an hour over the speed limit until her heart is pounding so fast she fears it will explode in her chest cavity. She manages alternating between rapid-fire piano scales—G Major, C Minor, A Minor Harmonic, broken and solid triads—and intense fiddling.

She pulls the car onto the shoulder, rests her head on the steering wheel for a long time and wonders where she's acquired the musical expertise to "play"? The following two days, she avows silence. On the third, she gives in and tries to speak, and although no words have returned, she discovers a lightness in her heart that she can still create music. The next moment she is sounding like two instruments at once—a violin, and is that an oboe? She laughs and it's a metal, clattering, melody of steel drums. For the rest of the week, Carole practises, not trying to speak, but attempting to add to her musical repertoire.

In front of her family, she does not make a peep. The boys continue to chatter—valiant stabs at filling her silence—news about school and friends. Finley drives himself through the household chores, stealing glances at her, staring when she permits, as if looking long enough at her will enable him to regenerate her lost voice. One night, Finley, lying in bed beside her, says, "I took out the garbage. I miss you asking me to do that every night." He sighs so deeply that Carole is moved to reach out to him . . .

Her moaning, gasping orgasmic release is expressed as several pipe organ chords, loud enough to rattle the windows, shrivel Finley inside her, and awaken the twins across the hall.

"Mom?" Ross calls out from their bedroom, then corrects himself, "Dad? What was that noise?"

Finley, panting and shaken, calls back to them, "Must be the wind or . . . I'll check. Go back to sleep." To Carole, he whispers, "Are you all right? Did I hurt you? It was too soon." He clasps her to himself as she begins to sob. Her breath catching in her throat sounds like strings being plucked on a harp. She tries to muffle them in Finley's shoulder. She hears the boys coming to their room. Finley fumbles for her nightie and slips it back over her head, pulls the covers around them.

Ross speaks into the darkness, "We're hearing music or something."

"Where's it coming from?" Robbie adds.

She stiffens in Finley's arms and tries to stifle herself.

"It's your mother," Finley replies, bewildered.

This sets Carole off louder than ever. The harp alternates with viola and bassoon.

Ross switches on the light and says, "Holy fffphh ...!"

Robbie says, "Co-o-ol!"

Finley grinds the heels of his hands into his eye sockets.

She wants them to understand what's happening to her, that she is not in control. It comes out like a pre-concert warm-up ... her thoughts flitting from one orchestral instrument in the pit to another.

The next day, Carole's mother arrives by taxi. As soon as she's seated, she lays her cane over her lap and says, "Carole, perhaps I have to take some of the blame for this. All those years you begged to take piano lessons with Mrs. Larder from next door. I used to walk into your bedroom and you'd be sitting by your window which opened onto Mrs. Larder's studio window, and you'd be listening to some other child playing their scales over and over again. And Mrs. Larder's voice, so pleasing, encouraging them. We never had the money for a piano or lessons. Perhaps I could have taken a job of some kind. But nonetheless, you're acting like a crazy person! Finley called me from work, distraught. What are the boys thinking of their mother? Buck up! You have duties here. It's hard, so very hard to say this to a daughter, but have you seen a psychiatrist yet?"

Carole is relieved her mother can't understand what she's trying to say to her. When her mother climbs back in a taxi, dazed and confused, however, Carole feels a surge of guilt anyway. She should not have directed those trombone blasts and sarcastic kazoo sounds at her.

Wendy and the girls from Stitch Club stop dropping in with their sympathetic casseroles when Carole attempts communication. Carole herself finds this falling off of social pressures a relief. She avoids Finley and the boys by pretending she's asleep when they arrive home in the evening. She hears Finley tell the boys that rest is the best cure. She is surprised a week later when the doorbell rings at noon one day, in the middle of her "movie overtures." Madame L'Heurtemps stands at the door with a red poinsettia in her hand. It reminds Carole she has done nothing to prepare for the holidays. How does one prepare without written lists? Perhaps she needs to further study Franz *Liszt*, she puns to herself. She still would not be ready for the holidays, but she might comprehend the difference between a symphonic poem and a symphony.

Madame L'Heurtemps sweeps into Carole's living room and beckons Carole to sit beside her. Madame begins, "I'm on a short lunch break, but I had to come. I feel so responsible for what happened; I take solace in the fact the police admitted the tuba may have inadvertently saved your life when it flipped on top of you. Sort of a protective shell, *n'est-ce pas?*"

Carole shrugs.

Madame L'Heurtemps continues, "My concerns now are regarding Ross. He has not been to music class all week. His practising had fallen off, but now he's skipping." She clears her throat. "It would be a second tragedy should Ross turn from music now." She continues when Carole cannot meet her eye. "Robbie has confided in me about your voice. I have spent two sleepless nights. I even called Klaus Loostroff to see if perhaps your meeting with him might bring on some psychological healing response. You were so mesmerized by him and the boys' performance that day, as I recall. Loostroff was no help. *Un homme terrible!* He said to me, 'What do you want me to do—hire her for my orchestra?' Fool! *Idiot!* Idiot!"

After taking a moment to compose herself, Madame L'Heurtemps says, "Do you mind if I listen?"

Carole's hand jerks out of her lap. She stops it before it reaches her throat. She does not want to *perform* for Madame L'Heurtemps.

"*S'il vous plaît?*" Madame L'Heurtemps coaxes.

Carole thinks about Ross, the sweet sound of his French horn. He always seemed the stronger of the two boys . . . until this. His life depends on structure and organization and this—what's happened to his mother—doesn't fit into the parameters of an orderly world. Robbie, on the other hand, so often lacking in self-discipline, is coping. Strange, how you think you know your children, but you can never know anyone. Perhaps them, least of all. You are blinded to who your children are by what you desire for them instead.

Madame L'Heurtemps breaks into her thoughts with applause. Carole doesn't realize she's been voicing them aloud. She is stunned to discover that she is composing three simple movements around a central theme. Her first original composition!

"Where's that from?" Madame L'Heurtemps hums the third movement, searching for its source.

Carole points to her head.

"You have been given such a gift! *Pourquoi? Pourquoi?*" Madame L'Heurtemps' voice trails off in awe. She begins again, "Have you ever contemplated what the human condition would be if we did not rely on the strictures of normality? Some think chaos. But here you are, outside what is normal—some would lock you up, treat you, burn you at the stake—and yet ... *Mon Dieu*, I didn't mean that ... but for whatever reason, you've been given a new voice. *Une voix distincte!* You must celebrate it."

Through the window, Carole watches Madame L'Heurtemps get into her car and drive away. She surges with gratitude and dismay at Madame's words. She lets the curtain fall shut. On a blank piece of paper, she begins with the five parallel lines to which she adds a treble clef, a time signature and then quarter and half notes. She stares at the round emptiness of the whole notes she completes. You can't fill the emptiness of a whole note, yet it's full when it's played. She realizes that she could fill her everyday life prior to the accident with chores and errands and lists—and still remain empty. Emptier than a whole note. She races through a page and then another. She starts to play. A piano sonata. Awkward and amateur, but listen, it exhibits standard form: exposition, development, recapitulation. She can't sit still for the excitement. She plays a slight variation of it, the struck strings responding inside her with satisfaction.

A celebration! Madame L'Heurtemps was right. Carole can't

wait for Finley and the boys to arrive home. She'll somehow convey that she wants to take them out for pizza, her first jaunt back into the outside world. While she is dressing, she hears her family come in the back door.

Finley is admonishing, "Keep your voice down."

Ross retaliates, "She'll be sleeping anyway. That's all she does now. Every night we come home, all she does is sleep!"

"You're being a jerk," Robbie stage-whispers.

"Well, if you hadn't blabbed to Madame L'Heurtemps, none of this would have happened. Nobody needed to know!"

Finley says, "Ross, sooner or later, other people are going to find out, especially if . . . if . . . her recovery isn't imminent. And what does Madame L'Heurtemps have to do with this anyway?"

Robbie blurts, "Ross has been skipping music class."

There is a short silence. Carol removes the blouse she has just put on and slides under the messy covers of her bed.

She hears Finley say, "And?"

"And nothing," Ross grinds out.

"And?" Finley reiterates.

"Madame L'Heurtemps stopped me in the hall this afternoon in front of my friends, telling me what an amazing gift Mom's been given. Some gift. She can't talk. All she can do is sound like a freakin' recording studio!"

"Ross!" Finley barks out.

"It's true!"

"That's enough, Ross!"

Ross rages, "My friends are like, 'What? Weird!'"

Finley lowers his voice. "Ross, it's hard on all of us right now. The doctor believes there's some neurological reason, even though it seems psychological . . . some post-traumatic stress or I don't know . . . we have to be patient. Once all the scans are done, maybe they can pinpoint—"

Ross yells, "I've heard this a hundred times."

Robbie responds, "Then give it a rest. You're acting like a loser. Why don't you think about Mom?"

"Why don't you shut up?"

Carole covers her mouth to keep from blurting out bagpipe wails from the bedroom.

"What if she never gets better?" Ross demands of Finley.

There is no response.

"Well, what if?" Robbie asks, his voice tentative.

Finley pauses, answers, "Then I guess we'll have to adjust."

"Adjust? Adjust? You're kidding?" Ross's voice wavers and squeaks, puberty peeling away. "Adjust to a mother who's a freak?"

"Dad," Robbie adds to his twin's outburst, "she can't stay like that!"

"Boys!" Finley snaps.

With Robbie in place as an ally, Ross has renewed strength. He refuses to stop. "It would have been better if she hadn't woken up from the coma if this is going to be our life now!"

"Go to your room, boys." Finley's voice is more sad than angry.

She clamps her eyes shut as her sons stomp past her doorway to their room. The house is filled with a silence, as in the moment after performance when the final notes fade ... drift over the audience ... and its members have to take a collective breath of comprehension before they can rise to their feet in thunderous ovation. The silent moment in her home stretches into several. Then she hears Robbie murmuring and what must be Ross's stifled sobs.

Their names return first, unbidden, back to her tongue before she can stop them. Quavering sounds, as if she's pronouncing them for the first time, naming her sons. The spoken words erupt from a shadowed place inside her: a place of sacrifice and burdened love that didn't exist before her children's birth. Carole won't forget how to play their names as melodies; but they will never appreciate this about her until she's gone.

Anytime You Think You Matter ...

BRIAN COMES HOME FROM A GRAVEYARD SHIFT ONE SUMMER morning, wakes me up as he slides into bed and says, "Jessica ... Coil Engholm's dead."

At first, in a half-sleep, the words don't affect me, as if Brian's said, "Damn crows ripped open the garbage bags." Then Coil's features flit in. I can't hold them all at once anymore, but I see Coil's lanky, springing step; his top lip slanting on its way to a grin; his eyes icing over after too many drinks; the magnetic north of his being on the first day of heavy snowfall that year, the first time I leaned into him and couldn't draw away, the scent of his suede jacket filling my nostrils and marking me.

Coil Engholm, you're only dead so that I have to think about you again.

"How?" I say, and my voice sounds shocked, my heart beats through my nightgown.

Brian gathers me in his arms, "Poor, crazy drunk choked on his own vomit in the jail cell."

I pull away. "What was he doing in jail?"

"Fernier picked him up on the street outside of Rachel and Roxy's place. That's what a couple of the guys were saying who came onto day shift this morning. They said Coil couldn't fit the key into the door of his truck. He kept lying down on the pavement beside the truck between attempts. Someone tried to get the keys off Coil, but he wouldn't give them up; they said he was still drinking from a mickey in his jacket pocket. The guys abandoned him eventually, went home to sleep. Roxy and Rachel saw Fernier pick him up."

"Why didn't Fernier drive Coil home?" I demand.

"Well, Christ, Jessica. He would have been worst off at home. If the guard hadn't gone for a piss, but old Jacobs . . . that bad prostate . . . it takes some effort to piss. I'm sure he was checking Coil every few minutes . . . conscientious old guy. And it's not Fernier's job to drive Coil twenty kilometres out to the swamp every time he's on a bender."

"Fernier won't have to worry about that anymore," I say and Brian goes silent.

I get out of bed and yank the curtains open. It's a perfect day outside. A cloudless sky. The mother robin flicks through the willow leaves with a fat worm. Cranking open the window, I hear the sound of the garbage truck moving down the street. The sound penetrates the room, touches the four walls, makes it clear that the world has not stopped. It hasn't even noticed. I think of Coil's parents, his four sisters, their husbands and kids. I wonder if it's garbage day on their streets. I imagine them gathered around the kitchen table, patting each other's hands and passing tissues, and I imagine myself in their circle. I could have been in that circle. Maybe Fernier is there, in his uniform, saying he's so sorry he didn't bring him to one of their places instead, and them all blaming themselves because they might not have opened their door at 2:00 in the morning for Coil if he was drunk again. And maybe one of them is thinking about me right now . . . how perhaps I could have tried harder, thinking if Jessica had been more of an adventurer, more willing to take risks, more of a woman.

Brian asks, "Jessica, you want me to take you out for breakfast?" He's sitting back up in bed, buttoning a shirt.

"No. Thanks," I say. "It's going to be too hot today for that shirt. You need some sleep."

Brian shrugs. "Unless there's a major breakdown, I've got nothin' much doing on tonight's shift."

Sometimes my body floods with appreciation for Brian's ultimate kindness. "Hard head, soft heart," my friend Lise is fond of saying about Brian. Other times, I can't shake the vague sensation that I've misplaced my love for Brian—like a missing car key—and can't recall where I left it. At this moment, I am incapable of discerning which of the two I feel.

I open the patio door and step out onto the screened deck Brian built this past spring, when the last of winter's thin, icy, snow still lay shaded beneath the lowest blue spruce branches. As he screwed two-by-fours down onto stringers and I came out to inspect his efforts, he said, "You'll be able to have coffee outside in your pyjamas all summer without a single, runny-nosed kid bringing you his ABC's to correct!" Though I dislike the way Brian always jokes about my students, the smell of freshly sawn wood made me feel carefree, and I laughed.

Carefree had never entered into the picture with Coil. "There's a reason his nickname rhymes with *turmoil*," my friend Lise once muttered. Lise was never in favour of my being with Coil. I suspected it was because she was in love with him herself at one time. Brian, who seldom talks about the past, mentioned once that every girl in high school had a crush on Coil Engholm. To Brian, that seemed to excuse my past involvement with him ... just something every girl in town had to go through. Was it envy or pity that Lise felt for me when I moved into town to accept my first teaching job and Coil staked a brief claim?

Coil is dead this morning. Why didn't I awaken knowing that? The phone is ringing and I know it's Lise on the other end. Brian seems to know too. He leaves it for me to answer in the kitchen.

"My gawd, Jess, did you hear?" Lise blurts out, exhaling a cigarette at the same time. She's supposed to be on the patch.

"About Coil?" I say.

"You heard." Her voice drops an octave.

Was she hoping to be the one to break the news? Or is she waiting for my reaction?

"I can't believe it," Lise says after several heartbeats of silence.

"Neither can I," I say and regret saying it. I don't want to slip into clichéd commiserating. The rest of the town will file out this morning, shake their heads, cluck their tongues, repeat the word *tragedy*. I want to feel something first. I want to remember Coil inside my body. Feel my heart split. Feel it heal. That's the least I can do for him . . . he's dead. A rush of anger spills into me like hot scalding water. Tears burn the edges of my eyes. I don't want Lise telling me what to feel next. I'm pissed off that she will hear my voice waver. I resent that she will say I owe Coil nothing without me having to ask her if I do. *It's been eight years*, Lise will say, *and he was never good to you, Jessica.*

"Jess," she says, "we should bake something to take to the Engholms. If Brian's sleeping, why don't you come over here?"

"He's not sleeping," I say. "He's making coffee." I catch Brian's eye as he measures scoopfuls. I notice the faint scar on his cheek and remember Brian telling me, on our wedding night, that he had been slashed by Coil Engholm's skate in a scramble in front of the net back in high school. That was the last time I remember Brian mentioning Coil's name until this morning.

Lise says, "Then I'll come there. I could use some coffee. I'm out of coffee here. Do you have chocolate chips?" Lise says, careful to sound sorrowful, but I'm certain she is too glad to absolve herself with a pan of baking.

Someone's dead, I want to remind her. I feel a sudden edginess, like if I don't hold on, my heart will start to swell like a balloon and float me upwards, float me to the end of the telephone cord. I force myself to focus on the dark liquid starting to drip from the coffee maker, its rude snorting noise, the normally delicious smell turned, this morning, too acrid. Lise says she's on her way, but I am meeting Coil for the first time.

I've come to this isolated, northern town from the big city to teach. Everywhere I look, there are endless tracts of trees, an evergreen eternity. From the beginning, it's as if the trees are responsible for the expanding emptiness I feel. A tree, a new hole, a tree, a new hole . . . like tree planters working a slope, planting loneliness inside me.

To fill the holes, I gravitate to what's familiar. I take a course. There aren't many courses available in Hematite. Someone has to drive in once a week from the campus in Thunder Bay to teach. That term they are offering business accounting and watercolour painting. A note tacked onto our staff room bulletin board also advertises, *Explore the Stars Seminars. Astronomy with Colin Engholm.* Lise, who is the secretary at my school, cautions against my enrolling, but we hardly know each other at the time and I ignore her advice.

Arriving at the first class, I take note of the other participants: a pair of high school students; one elderly man who fiddles with his hearing aid; two women who think they've registered for an astrology course, but stay on anyway; a man in his mid-thirties who reveres UFO's and hums the *Close Encounters* notes to himself when he looks through the telescope; one middle-aged woman who doesn't care a stick for stars, but gets away from her husband for the evening. I am an alien on the brink of fleeing. Colin Engholm—or Coil, as he insists we call him—holds me in place with his piercing stare.

The classes are held out at "the swamp," Coil's name for his place in the bush. He has a quaint log cabin, somehow sparse and cluttered at the same time. He has a 16-inch reflector telescope. On the clear nights we spend the three hours outside; when it's cloudy, we sit at the rough, pine dining table and study star charts or discuss theories of the universe's birth. Coil's teaching style is that of the spark at the end of a dynamite fuse. No one is bored.

On the night of the fourth class, heavy snow falls; the highway is packed with icy slush and I'm the only one who drives the twenty kilometres. When Coil sees me at his door, a grin slides onto his face and he says, "What did you think we were going to see tonight, Jessica?"

I say, "I thought we'd . . . we'd be doing theory?"

He shakes his head, "Don't they close the highways where you come from?"

"The highway is closed?"

"Will be. Temperature's dropping," he says, while I stand there, the snow pelting me, melting on my embarrassment.

I say, "Well, then, I'd better head back while I can."

Coil reaches for a jacket, "You'll stay put," he insists. "No one dies on the ice on my watch."

I feel too stupid to argue, though I'm wondering where I'm to sleep and how I'm to get to work in the morning. I follow him as he springs past me towards the shore of the nearby lake. He points at the sky and I look up. In the faint light from the cabin, I see the spikes of snow driving down towards my eyes.

"Like a zillion shooting stars," Coil says. "You know what was unique about the first astronauts who orbited and took photographs of Earth from space? They had the advantage of looking down and realizing the same thing as we do when we look up . . . that each of us is sweet-dick-all in the big picture. I learned that one cold night when the sky was plastered with stars. Anytime you think you matter, Jessica . . . just look up."

He chooses that moment to run out onto the thin shoreline ice. I hear it creak and crackle, like a grinding of back molars.

"What are you doing?" I yell.

"The trick is to stay ahead of it. Keep yourself light, like you're flying."

I run alongside the lake and when he comes close enough, I grab for his arm that's spread open like a wing. He leaps back to shore, toppling me off balance, landing me in the wet snow. He hauls me to my feet, and I am so close to him, I can't pull myself away.

I say, "You're insane!"

He says, "I thought you were a teacher?"

"I am a teacher!"

"Oh, oh! You are a teacher. In that case teach me something about myself I don't already know."

I am wet, shivering, and exasperated at his childish taunt. "Well, for starters," I say, "our lives must be for something, or else why are we living them?"

"Why indeed?" he says. "I think we've lived our lives to culminate in this moment." He leans to kiss me, but he breaks away and says, "Because I was about to take off and fly, and if you hadn't been here to prevent me, then men would be birds, wouldn't they?"

When I sleep with him that first night, there are feathers and wings and updrafts, and only a hint of beer on his breath.

I spend the better part of the following year thinking I can keep him on the ground. More often than not, he takes off for Rachel and Roxy's place, the sisters with the non-stop party ability. I try accompanying Coil for the first while. It makes me long for my companions from the astronomy class. Sometimes, when the party is in full swing—Roxy passing salt, lemons and a tequila bottle, the stereo speakers pounding out laryngitis-bound bands, the names of which I don't recognize, and Rachel locking the back bedroom behind her accompanied by somebody who won't bother to remove his baseball cap—I ask Coil if he's ready to leave. When he focuses on me long enough to determine what I'm asking, I see that I repulse him. Yet, strangely, we continue. My willingness to be such a dupe must make me endearing as well. I learn to store humiliation in my hip pocket—that way it's always on me.

Near the end, he says, "Look, there's nothing going on between me and any of them. They just understand."

"Coil, I could understand too, if you let me. You're so bent on destroying."

"Jessica, I don't comprehend it, myself. One morning after, I woke and someone had changed the rule book."

I spend a month of my summer vacation back at my parents' home. When I return to Hematite, Coil stays sober for a whole week. I ask him what brought on the change, hoping he'll admit he loves me. Instead, he says, "Jessica, the underside of this town is like the bloated belly of a dead fish." Careful not to reveal my disappointment, I plan a celebratory dinner, invite a few friends from work, find recipes for mocktails. We eat, swim, play Trivial Pursuit, and I fail to notice Coil getting blitzed until it's too late. By the end of the following week, Coil has drifted so far away I can no longer reach that high. Our relationship ends without acknowledgement: no last-ditch effort to save it, no final scene to mark its demise.

Coil is dead. Where did his wild energy go? Has it been converted to the electrical impulses that are generating my thoughts; remembering—in the time it takes to brew a pot of coffee—the better part of a year, and how someone who mocks your love for them can hollow you out more than any tract of trees? Is it Coil's energy that brings Lise into my kitchen brandishing a brown paper bag in her hand? Inside is a bottle of coffee liqueur, half full. I expect her to hug me in some exchange of sympathies. I won't hug her back, I decide. She walks right past me and hands the bottle to Brian.

He looks at the liqueur, says, "Seems strangely fitting, Lise. But, cripes, I can't remember the last time I drank at breakfast." He pours out three mugs of coffee and adds a couple of glugs to each.

Lise tastes it, smacks her lips. "The last time I spoke to him was the night he crashed your wedding reception."

Brian snorts. "You were pretty feisty, wrestling that microphone out of his hands."

"Well, the two of you were looking stunned in the middle of your first waltz with Coil trying to stop the proceedings," Lise says and laughs.

I say, "How can you laugh about that? It was my wedding day."

Lise and Brian look at each other and laugh harder. Then they carry the coffee pot and liqueur bottle out onto the screened deck.

For a moment I remain in the kitchen, refusing to join them. I'm hearing Coil's slurred words at the front of the Legion Hall. *I can tell you the bride's made a mistake. Married the wrong guy. Brian, Brian, sorry, buddy, but you're . . .* , and here he seems to lose his train of thought as he watches Lise and Brian's brother descending on him, then he refocuses and says, . . . *you're chicken shit, Brian! She needs someone who can fly her to the moon!*

Brian's brother hauls Coil out of the building and the DJ—who is not from Hematite, but who has the microphone back in his hand—says to applause and whistles, *Some guys are really, really sore losers, eh?*

I am standing there in my puffy white gown, with my veil wrapped around my arm to keep it from getting soiled on the floor of the Legion Hall, ashamed to be wishing I'd known earlier in the afternoon that there was a contest; ashamed to have my pulse throbbing with the thrill of my wedding guests witnessing not my vows, but Coil's opinion that I deserved better.

I hear Brian say to Lise, out on the deck, "He should never have come back to Hematite."

Lise agrees. "Do you think he had to sacrifice his own future to make amends for Streak?"

There is a silence as I stand at the sliding door to the deck. I see Brian shrug. "Who knows what Coil was thinking in that saturated brain of his?"

I take a drink from my doctored coffee and grimace. "Who's Streak?"

Lise looks at me. "Who's Streak?" she repeats.

Brian says, "You never heard of Streak, Gerry Abbotsford?"

They exchange looks as I take another gulp of my coffee. Brian mutters, "Christ, you moved in with Coil for a while, didn't you?"

I go out onto the deck then and pretend something interests me in the tract of trees beyond our back yard.

"Rhetorical question," Lise says to Brian. "Give her a break. Did you tell her about Streak? Did I?"

Brian reaches down beside his chair and adds straight liqueur to his mug. I peer at him, more concerned with his behaviour than the identity of Streak for the moment.

Brian notices my raised eyebrow, sighs, begins, "Coil and Streak were the biggest hockey stars in this town. They were both applying to a university in the States, practically assured of scholarships after they cinched the provincial title. The rest of us on the team were bystanders with Coil in net and Streak playing forward. Coach's instructions for three years were *Feed the puck to Streak*, and *Don't screen Coil*".

Lise snorts at this, "If Streak didn't get a hat trick in a game, the rest of you had to come early to practice. If Coil didn't get a shut-out, it was extra dry-land man-makers."

I stare at them. "You won a provincial hockey championship with Coil?!"

"I rounded out the bench," Brian answers.

"Well . . . still," I say, "why have you never mentioned it? Where's your trophy?"

"Some of us leave some things behind, Jessica. Others don't . . . or can't."

There is a long pause, in which the flutter of the robins' wings in the willow tree can be heard.

Lise urges him to continue.

Brian begins again. "Right after we won the championship, Streak and Coil organized the victory party. A bunch of us snow-mobiled out to the dam, lit a bonfire, started drinking."

"I was there," Lise says, "and Roxy and Rachel, quite a few others. It was freezing cold that night. Too cold for the beginning of April; we'd already had a thaw. We didn't expect the cold."

Brian adds, "It was late. We'd had too many beers. Coil decided we should take the shortcut home across the lake."

Lise interjects, "It was Brian who resisted and said No. Some of us thought it was an okay idea. We wanted to get home where it was warm. But Brian said he knew the middle of the lake was open water."

"There was an allegiance between Streak and Coil," Brian says.

"Yeah," Lise agrees. "It wasn't as if Streak was stupid. He just didn't seem to have a need for his own brain when the two of them were together, because Coil's was always into overtime."

"I still remember Streak saying to me that night, *We're not going to the middle of the lake, asshole,* and then him looking to Coil for approval."

Lise interjects, "Brian, you managed to convince the rest of us it wasn't safe, despite the two of them hassling you. We're lucky we listened. It wasn't easy to defy them even though we resented them dominating our lives."

Brian continues, "Coil and Streak took off. We put out the bonfire and set out on the longer trail around the lake. We didn't know about the accident until morning. It was Fernier, first year on the job. He came to all our houses before he put together his report."

Lise finishes for him, "Streak's snowmobile went through the ice. Nobody can figure how Coil saved his life, how his own machine didn't go down, how he managed to drive into town being wet himself from hauling Streak out of the water. Streak was unconscious from hypothermia by the time Coil got him to the hospital. He lost all his fingers on one hand, and most of one foot. Some people wanted to get Coil awarded a medal for bravery for saving Streak's life, but one day that summer before the official ceremony, Streak started his dad's car in the garage with the door closed." Lise stops here, downs the contents of her mug.

Brian says, "It was hot that day, just like today."

"What did Coil do?" I ask.

Brian says, "He went to the States, got suspended from the university team for drinking in the first season, came back to Canada and drank his way through a few more years on campus. Maybe if he'd stayed away from Hematite, but his family was here ..."

Brian says, "I'm surprised he didn't tell you about Streak. You lasted longer than any of the others."

"I'm not surprised," I say. *Anytime you think you matter, Jessica ...*

I try to look up, but the sunlight is too blinding above. Instead, I'm forced to focus on what's directly in front of me, here on this deck. The robins flickering by, the attempting to make sense of loss, the second offer for breakfast out ... these are small gauges for mattering.

Acknowledgements

I would like to acknowledge the Manitoba Arts Council and the Manitoba Writers' Guild for their past assistance. Numerous members of the Selkirk Literary Guild, including founder Terry Lulashnyk, offered me their support and valued critiques. The extra phone calls, emails and tea times with writing friends Sheila McClarty, laureen grant and Deborah Froese held the inevitable isolation at bay. For their encouraging words of earlier days, thanks to Jake MacDonald, Margaret Sweatman and Clarise Foster. Thanks also to Turnstone's Todd Besant, Sharon Caseburg and Kelly Stifora for their guidance and generosity; and to Heidi Harms, Terry Gallagher and Fiona Irvine-Goulet for their added expertise. I will always be grateful to my editor, Wayne Tefs, who over the years assured me this could be done, and periodically took time out to reveal the way. Thanks to my parents for my education and their love. A special thank you to my husband, David, whose unwavering optimism keeps me afloat; and to my children, Phil and Miranda, who make it all worthwhile.

A version of "Jackpot Jungle" originally appeared in *Prairie Fire*; "Too Much Beauty . . . Is Curse" in *Under the Prairie Sky Anthology*; and "What Jeanie and Ella Canned" in *Other Voices*. I am grateful to the judges and editors of these publications.